Weathering the Storm

By Suzie Bronk Hunt

Weathering the Storm

Copyright © 2018   Suzie Bronk Hunt

All rights reserved.

ISBN-13: 9781090640550

***

Weathering the Storm is a work of fiction. Rienville is an imaginary town filled with imaginary citizens. Any resemblance to actual places, events and people is entirely happenstance.

***

Book Cover Art by Lori Gomez

Weathering the Storm

With Gratitude

Thanks to all those who have weathered the storms of life
with me.
Especially my husband Jay and our children,
Jennifer and Jay Dee.

You are all special blessings in my life.

Weathering the Storm

Table of Contents

1 - Prologue

5 - Tropical Storm Stella

20 - Hurricane Stella

63 – Category 2

134 - Landfall

145 - Tropical Depression Stella

Prologue

A Wednesday Night in April

Dice clicked as they rolled across the tables, with the occasional outburst when three of a kind turned up. Conversations overlapped in the living room while the women were intent on each roll. The monthly bunko game had been floating from house to house for nineteen years.

Most of the players were originals, natives of Rienville while a few had joined up when others had moved or had exhibited the ultimate bad form to die. The women gathered monthly to unwind and hear about life in their town.

"Our office manager says the Navy's got a new research program coming into the space center," said Katie Woodruff, as she sipped her drink and waited for the three die to move to her side of the table.

Rose Marino leaned in at the news. As a realtor, any new project at the NASA facility just over the Mississippi border from Rienville, meant new people moving to the area and in need of homes.

"Really," Rose murmured casually as she tossed the dice and came up with one '6' out of the three. She picked them up and rolled again. No winners appeared on that roll and she passed the dice to Ellen sitting on her left.

"Something about underwater robots and water currents. That's all I really remember her saying. Sounds like a big project," Katie said.

Rose marked, 'call about new research program' on her mental To Do list for the next day and concentrated on the action in front of her. If she could get the name and contact information for the project manager, Rose of Wisteria Realty Group could make the move for their new employees to the area very easy and land some nice commissions at the same time.

This wasn't the first lucrative tip Rose had picked up during the seemingly innocuous bunko games. Births, deaths, affairs, along with new businesses, and proposed parish regulations, were all food for conversation when these women got together.

Conversations flowed freely following dinner and play resumed. As the women rolled, the stress from their jobs and families took a backseat to the news of the day and laughter. Katie, like many of the others, came mainly for the laughter. Winning the cash pot was secondary.

The original twelve players had been a homogeneous group, formed from young mothers needing a night away from toddlers, housework and husbands who brought their own issues home from work. As the children grew up, more of the players took jobs outside the home, if not for the money, for the mental stimulation.

And as the years passed, the people in the seats changed. The bunko group became more of a hodgepodge of women with varied backgrounds. Local economics changed. Although there were a few homemakers still among the regulars, their numbers also included Joyce the bus driver, Deb the teacher, Ruth the children's court advocate and Charlotte, owner of a po-boy shoppe.

The bell at the head table rang and the round ended. Rose and Katie, as winners, moved to the head table and sat down with Magen Hoops and Lola Normandy. Along with Rose, Lola was one of Katie's closest friends. Magen and Lola were on a roll, figuratively speaking, and had been at the head, or winners table, for the past three rounds.

Katie Woodruff was a newbie, new to bunko and new to Rienville. Raised in Wisconsin, she had followed her heart and a man to Louisiana about a year ago. When he continued on to the next job, Katie wasn't in the passenger seat. The details were still sketchy on why things played out that way. In many ways, the women at bunko had become a free support group for her and the monthly dice games helped heal her heart. Dealing with lost love and amended dreams were specialties with this group of street corner therapists.

"Welcome to the winner's circle. Don't plan on staying," Lola said as the two women sat down. Rose moved the bowl of M&Ms, a requisite for each month's host to provide, to the other side of the table. Although she had a quirky habit to only eat the red ones, temptation was temptation.

Weathering the Storm

"I believe you two have gotten too comfortable siting here. I see an opportunity to stretch your legs coming in the next few minutes," Rose said, the laugh lines around her eyes crinkling.

Lola played with the dice, waiting for the other women to finish refilling their glasses and sit down. She was not one of the original members of the group, but almost. She was invited to be a substitute for a player within a year of the group starting and that was her role for a few years. When someone, she couldn't remember her name anymore, moved away, Lola was invited to take her place and be a regular.

"That's right," said Lola, "We're smoking, and Megan's got three bunkos already so beware."

Lola saw the last person sitting down across the living room and rang the small, brass bell on their table, starting the latest round. Dice immediately started clicking as they tumbled across the card table tops.

"Those guys in Colorado are calling for another busy season," said Lola. Watching the dice, her hand poised to try and capture the dice if three of the coveted number made an appearance.

"I really wish they'd just shut up and leave it alone. When they start that crap, people start double thinking on buying a new house," said the resident realtor, as she rolled. Getting no points, she passed the dice to Katie.

The hurricane gurus in Colorado had released their annual hurricane forecast. Once again, they were calling for tough times along the Gulf Coast.

"Sitting up in the mountains, I don't think they realize what damage they do when they release that report. What do they really know anyway?" said Joyce, commenting from the next table. Like any weather forecast, the reports were guesses and not very accurate. The anxiety they caused was hard on some. For most of the women there that night, the forecasts were ignored for now. They had been through enough storms and evacuations and knew there was nothing to do but be ready to leave town between the months of June and October.

"Whether their guesses say five storms or 50, it's not going to make anyone around here prepare any more than they do already," said Joyce.

Katie had arrived in town late in the year and had only experienced a brush with a tropical storm during her first hurricane season last fall. She hadn't been through a full-fledged category storm scenario yet and that was fine by her.

"I say ignore them and don't worry about things until you need to," said Lola as she reached for the dice. "My aunt Helen used to say, 'Don't put up your umbrella before it starts to rain.' Wise woman, my Aunt Helen," finished Lola as she wrote three tick marks on her sheet.

Someone across the room shrieked with a lucky roll of the dice. Katie picked up the cubes and continued her elusive quest for her first bunko for the night.

23.0N (Latitude), 84.0W (Longitude). 40 MPH. 606 miles southeast of Rienville, LA.

Satellite imagery indicates that a tropical depression has strengthened and is now Tropical Storm Stella. Maximum sustained winds are estimated to be 40 mph with higher gusts. Continued strengthening is expected. Updates to follow. National Hurricane Center – National Oceanic and Atmospheric Administration (NOAA).

"Well, that's just great!"

Lying in bed, having clicked on the Weather Channel, Rose listened to the latest report on what was now been named Tropical Storm Stella. Winds barely topping 40 mph, Stella was still a literal tempest in Rose's small corner of the real estate world.

It's too early to call Craig and Becky. Rose would have to wait until after 8 a.m. Their dream of home ownership would be delayed. She had forewarned the newlyweds of this possibility. Early September was traditionally when hurricane season started to crank up. As smart as the young couple was, her clients didn't always listen to information they didn't like.

Turning off the TV, her dogs stretched under the comforter before emerging. They left for the kitchen to start their morning routine of milk bones and daily medicine. Rose made a quick trip into the bathroom to brush her teeth, push a brush through her still sandy brown hair and pulled it back into a ponytail. After slipping on her favorite flannel pants with moose on them, she was ready to meet the herd in the kitchen. She could hear them 'talking' to each other, whining and carrying on due to their perceived lack of sustenance. Their patience was waning as she headed to the kitchen. Rose knew patience was not in their doggie vocabulary.

Her mangy, but lovable, crew looked like the old joke of what's black and white and red all over. They were all rescues from the pound or the roadside: black lab mix Gertie Mae; Butch the snowy white mutt with a bulldog in his past, and Ruby, the hound whose shiny coat lived up to her name. When she entered the room, they sat waiting in the middle of the kitchen floor like statues. After dispensing the meds and food bowls, silence reigned again.

Rose grabbed the pad of paper on the counter and started to rewrite her to do list for the day. Once Stella had gotten her name and crossed that imaginary line at latitude 20.0, longitude 80.0, most if not all closings in the real estate market went on hold. No insurance company wanted to take on new liability in the face of a storm so she would be in the proverbial holding pattern with the Higgins closing until Stella dropped in somewhere along the gulf coast and went inland.

As she got a jelly jar out of the cupboard and poured herself a glass of orange juice, Rose looked out the window at the dazzling blue sky and started her vigil for Stella.

23.5N, 84.0W. 40 MPH. 582 miles southeast of Rienville.

It was two days past the expected date for the secretary at the oncologist's office to call back with the results. Katie willed the cell phone in her pocket to buzz.

Katie, born Mary Katherine but only her mother called her that when she was really angry, stared at the computer monitor in her cubicle. She sat waiting for the new data set she had entered to be saved. While work should be the priority, the small phone in her scrubs pocket kept stealing her attention.

Her annual check-up two weeks before had started out routinely when she saw Dr. Pichon. After dispensing with the usual half-truths about her diet and exercise regime, the manual breast exam proved to be anything but routine.

"Have you noticed anything unusual during your monthly checks," Dr. Pichon asked while she palpated one particular spot. To Katie, the doctor seemed to be checking that area with more than the normal interest.

"No, not really," she said. "I'm really not good at doing self-exams." Katie's breathing quickened as her doctor continued to work on that side.

"No burning, soreness, swelling?"

"No, nothing." She tried to read the doctor's face for clues to why all the questions.

"Ok then," said Dr. Pichon. "Nothing to get excited about. I feel an unusual spot here." She took Katie's hand and guided it to her lower left breast. Trying hard to feel it, while at the same time wishing anything there into oblivion, Katie let the physician move her hand to the area in question.

"Probably nothing, but I still would feel better if we get it checked out," she said, moving to the counter to make notes in Katie's file. "I'll write you up for a mammogram and we'll go from there."

With that said, they lapsed into a quiet time while Dr. Pichon finished the rest of the annual exam. Katie looked at the nurse in the room and took solace in that she fact that the woman showed no signs of concern as she handed the doctor what she needed.

Filling out paperwork to get her in the door at the imaging center, the physician kept a pleasant expression and her tone calm. Handing Katie the sheet, she said, "take this out to the nurses' desk and she'll help you make the appointment. The sooner we know what, if anything is a problem, the better. Any questions?"

Katie had many, many questions, but she couldn't come up with a single coherent one at the moment.

"No. She hugged the gown closed and stepped off the table to get dressed.

"I know it is easier said than done Katie, but there's no use worrying about something until you know you have something to worry about," the doctor said kindly, as she squeezed Katie's arm. "We'll call as soon as we have the results of the scans." With a small smile, the doctor wished her a good weekend as she passed through the door.

Have a good weekend,' Katie thought as she pulled on her pants. '*Like that's going to happen*' she mumbled as she worked on the zipper.

That had been two weeks ago. She got lucky to get a mammogram scheduled fairly quickly at the local hospital. That day, Katie endured what, from previous experience, were a high number of scans on her left breast. She had promised herself a big, chocolate malt if she didn't scream at the technician to quit making that final adjustment and just hit the damn button.

Deep breaths and thoughts of chocolate definitely helped during the uncomfortable procedure.

After getting dressed, the technician asked if she would have a seat in the consultation room.

Don't panic yet Katie girl. Now Katie was a little nervous. Usually she left immediately with the comment that she'd receive a card in the mail after the radiologist had a chance to review the scans. Then again, this wasn't a screening mammogram.

A short, perky young woman with her blond hair cut in a smart style walked in. She was wearing the requisite white coat and it sported buttons with funny sayings on her lapel.

Weathering the Storm

Smiling at Katie, she held out a hand and introduced herself as Dr. Amber Stone. Katie returned the smile as she shook her hand and watched as the doctor sat down behind the desk.

"Okay, let's cut to the chase as I am sure that's what you want to hear right now," the doctor said looking up from the digital photos sitting on the desk. "You've got a small mass in your left breast, about five centimeters in diameter. I only see one. Sorry for all the extra squeezes in there. We wanted to make sure there weren't any others lurking in there and you've got a lot of fibrous tissue."

The doctor paused to take a breath. Katie felt like there was no air left in the room for her. She made the effort to continue to breathe normally.

"From these scans, we can't tell if it is benign or not." Katie further stiffened in her chair and her eyes grew wide. *This woman could use some work on her bedside manner.*

"Your next step is a needle biopsy so they can remove some of the cells from the growth and check them out. It could be a benign cyst, or a tumor and we won't know until they look at the cells," the radiologist paused, giving Katie a moment to let that sink in.

"Do you understand what I've told you so far?" the physician asked.

Katie wondered what her facial expressions told the doctor as she absorbed the news.

Katie nodded her head slowly and then produced a quiet "yes". Katie could feel pressure building behind her eyes. Her mantra in her head became *'No tears'*. She would not cry in front of the doctor. Katie tried to focus on the good. It wasn't the doctor's fault the news was not better.

"If you agree to the needle biopsy, we will get it scheduled as soon as possible. It's a fairly quick procedure done with a local anesthetic. You'll leave with just a Band-aid." As far as Katie knew, nothing involving the words 'biopsy' and 'anesthesia' was ever easy. She appreciated their efforts to act quickly and that snapped her to attention.

"I want it done as soon as possible. Where do I go?" said Katie, shifting to the front of the hard chair. She realized the doctor appeared to be only slightly older than her. *It can't be fun handing out news like this.*

"Now don't be concerned over the name, but I'd like to recommend you to the hospital's cancer center for the biopsy. The have an in-house lab that can do the cell work and it wouldn't have to be sent out for processing. That should make the process easier and get you your results faster."

Cancer center. No tears. No tears.

Katie looked at the woman sitting across from her. *She really does seem concerned about me.* It warmed Katie's heart while making her a little scared at the same time. Looking the doctor in the eye, she did her best to put a hopeful look on her face.

"Let's do this. Make the appointment." Her small smile was slowly fading, and she could feel the tears pushing to get out. She'd hold them in until she got to the car. If she could get to the car soon.

Dr. Stone came around the desk and squeezed Katie's shoulder. Hunching down to meet her patient eye to eye, she laid a hand on Katie's forearm.

"As of this moment, there is nothing that says this growth is bad news. It could be no news and be benign. Hold on to that until we know one way or another, Okay?"

Looking back at her, Katie nodded and then looked down at her hands, continuing to nod.

Dr. Stone patted her forearm again before rising. "I'll write up the order. Just give me a few minutes."

Katie nodded again and heard the door close quietly behind her.

No tears.

23.6N 84.1W. 40 MPH. 573 miles southeast of Rienville.

"Come on Pop," Lola spoke into the phone while she got out the flashlights and checked the batteries. *Why do I always wait to do something so simple until the lines at Wal-Mart would be a mile long.*

"No need just yet" James said. "Spot and I are just going to sit and watch the cloud banks go by." Lola knew that Spot, his father would describe the black lab mix as 'just one big spot', was probably lounging in front of the sliding glass doors, watching the egrets' fish across the bayou. It was his second favorite spot at the camp. The first was anywhere Lola's father was.

"The models say Stella could make a run for our coast. You need to take this seriously," she said.

"I'm watching the signs. So far, so good. No need to leave yet."

Lola's father and his trusty companion lived sixteen feet above the ground in his converted retirement camp on the edge of Bayou Oiseaux and the Lefleur Wildlife Management area. If Stella was a weak storm, his home should be fine. There would be no getting him out due to high water. Although her father was in good shape for 82, she didn't relish the prospect of having to get to him by boat if there was an emergency.

"You'd be more comfortable here and you can visit with the kids," Lola tried. She knew bantering with his granddaughter was always an enticing prospect for James. "You know the power will go out, big storm or little storm."

"We didn't have electricity until I was fourteen so I think I can survive. Now let me go so I can check on my supplies."

Lola told him she loved him, would talk to him soon and rang off.

She imagined him going onto his deck, looking over the weather-beaten railing at the water, checking the level against the cypress tree trunks along the banks and making plans. While the terns and fish crows flew overhead, he would check on the hand crank on his boat lift that could lower his boat to the water, even after the power went out.

*

Lola knew her father very well. James headed out the door overlooking the bayou and climbed down to where the boat winch was located. James moved well for his age. Hard work all his life and a stubborn exercise ethic learned during his navy days helped him still feel like a man 20 years younger. If someone asked, James would give much of the credit to his late wife Audrey for taking a lot of the mundane, day to day worries off his shoulders. He hadn't really known how heavy that burden was until she died.

There was a cut in from the bayou's main channel that ran underneath his house. As James checked the lift cables, he made plans to move his SUV to higher ground, such as it was in southeast Louisiana, and return by water. It was there that James could park his boat and winch it up to sit snug under the house for safe keeping. That contingency was not something he liked to think about, but he was prepared.

Once the storm passed, even when the roads were flooded, James would lower the boat again and he would check on Ms. Beryl and his other neighbors down the bayou.

Just him and Spot, he thought looking out over the water and marsh grass along the shore. They'd be floating on the waves. Right now, the breeze was pleasant, ruffling the grass and sending ripples along the top of the bayou.

He looked down. *It would be a good time to pull up the crab traps. No use in losing them in the coming surge. Maybe there's enough for a dinner with Ms. Beryl.* Always a pleasant thought.

James walked toward the stairs as his four-legged shadow rose from the wood dock to follow.

24.2N, 84.4W. 50 MPH. 529 miles southeast of Rienville.

Rose went to her office. A light breeze ruffled her hair as she got out of her car. The sky overhead was the color of a blue raspberry snowball. No one was there but her. She could get work done at home, but she might be stuck there for a few days and she was bad about getting cabin fever.

The old building creaked from a sudden gust as the winds had started to increase. She grabbed the door to keep it from banging on the wall when the wind caught it. There were a few gusts here and there. The office had been part of Rienville's city center since before people started naming storms to keep track of which one went where. She gained comfort knowing the solid wood floors and old fireplace had stood strong since the building was built before the turn of the last century.

Maybe we won't have to run from this storm. Rose pressed send on an e-mail updating a client on their home's sale schedule. Turning away from her computer monitor, she watched leaves from the live oak outside her office swirl in a mini cyclone before landing in the vacant lot next door.

Each storm in their vicinity of the Gulf of Mexico required a decision.

This decision would have to wait a little longer though. One of her husband's favorite sayings came to mind. "Is this the hill you want to die on?" That became all too real for many during Hurricane Katrina.

As much as she hated packing and loading up the car, Rose hated the waiting more. She felt her shoulders start to tighten. That's where she felt stress first. By the time Stella made landfall, she'd have to have Patrick work on the kinks in her neck as well as her shoulders. She clicked on an icon on the corner of her computer screen and saw the NOAA weather map take over the screen. The cones of possibility came up and the model trajectories squiggled across the Gulf like something a preschooler drew.

The models, as usual at this stage of the game, were having the storm go literally a dozen different directions. The hot pink line had Stella headed for Tampa, the green toward the Sabine River on the Texas border. The rest of the lines, mimicking the colors of a rainbow, fell somewhere in between.

Models, what do they really know this early out? Rose had visions of meteorologists drawing random lines with pretty markers on a board during happy hour at the weather office. Looking at the jumbled mess on her screen, she thought they might already be at a bar. Her lips turned up at the corners as she thought of a bunch of tipsy weathermen.

"Troublemakers," she mumbled to her empty office. Rose pulled up another storm tracking website on her computer screen.

"Come on west side," Rose emphasized her words with a little cheer. The weaker side would have lower waves and less slosh factor on the bayous. Better yet, Stella could make a hard-left turn and head west toward Galveston. A little south of that city and it would bypass major population centers and head into the desert. Kick a little Texas drought butt in the process.

For all her positive thoughts and little cheers at her computer screen, according to the crayon artwork there, Stella was still heading toward the Big Easy.

Sipping her diet soda, Rose picked up the phone to talk to her first client of the day.

*

Spot sat in the doorway, watching the water. Every few minutes, she looked at James and cocked her head, one ear flipped up.

"I'm with you sweetie. Should we worry?" James often talked out conundrums with Spot.

Putting her snout up into the air, Spot sniffed and sneezed. James had picked up some unusual smells on the winds, coming from the water.

Weathering the Storm

The dog moved along the railing and repeated the sniffing process. Her tail moved down and under her rear end.

Looking back at his constant companion, James stilled. Did Spot smell trouble brewing?

Dogs can be damned perceptive. James leaned over the railing and looked down at the current moving past the camp.

Taking a last sniff next to the open patio doors, Spot shuffled inside. Moving to her dog couch, complete with arm rests, she lowered her lanky body into the comfortable cushions. Tucking in her front paws under her chest, the breeze from the doorway lightly ruffled her fur and moved the papers on the coffee table beside the dog's bed. Spot laid her head on one of the arm rests and watched James for a few moments before drifting off to sleep.

Her owner sat in his recliner and reached over to stroke the dog's fur. He felt comfort in the silkiness of her coat as he watched the clouds float north through the open door.

24.0N, 84.4W. 60 MPH. 541 miles southeast of Rienville.

Later that day and sitting in her home office, Rose turned down the radio and marked the coordinates with her ultra-fine green sharpie. It was a ritual with her, tracking each storm 'til it made landfall. At the start of June every year, she'd get one of the free hurricane maps distributed at the hardware store. Rose would take it down to the print shop in Olde Towne to be laminated, then sit back and wait for storm season to start

Looking at the map, Rose realized her husband thought it was a bit silly. But he would still remind her that the tropics report was fixing to come on the Weather Channel at 10 minutes before the hour when he knew she wanted to extend the line on her map.

Her cell phone rang from where it sat on the kitchen counter.

Drat, I hate it when I set it down and then leave the room. She trotted down the hall. She knew the ringtone. It was the sound of bullets hitting a metal target. Yes, that would be her husband.

"Hey," she said, catching it on the last ring before it went to voicemail.

"What's the news at hurricane central? Time to think about bugging out?"

"So far, so good," she said. "Stella's still weak." As the 19th named storm of the year, they had had this conversation often over the past few months.

"If you think it's heading this way, let me know," he replied. Without an imminent departure, Patrick was already concentrating on the next repair request at his gunsmith shop.

"Don't I always. Hurricane Central out." She heard his smile as he disconnected the call.

The Marino household did not leave when smaller storms came calling. Not at least since the kids grew up and moved out. Patrick was not averse to leaving for a category 2 storm or bigger. But if they left, Patrick liked to leave early. The idea of getting stuck on the interstate with a few thousand yahoos who waited until the last minute to leave

Weathering the Storm

New Orleans was not pleasant. Rose knew all the dog friendly places on their route north. Once they made the decision, Rose and Patrick tended to leave ahead of the crowd and made it more of a fun mini-vacation than an evacuation.

24.3N, 84.4W. 60 MPH. 524 miles southeast of Rienville.

Katie listened to the post-biopsy instructions from the nurse and tried to think positive thoughts. The procedure had not been as bad as she thought it would be. Katie was glad she had got the last appointment for the day and didn't have to go back to work. She didn't feel like putting on a cheery face at the moment.

"Keep the area clean, take Tylenol for any soreness, call if the area turns red, feels hot or you have a fever in the next 24 hours" The nurse rattled off the list without looking at the papers in her hand.

Pretty straight forward stuff. Katie folded the instruction sheet the nurse handed her and stuffed it into her pocket as she was left alone to dress.

After she put her bra on and pulled her t-shirt over her head, Katie grabbed her purse and opened the door to the examination room. The nurse was waiting with a release form and checked her contact information.

"How soon will I hear something?" Katie asked. *30 minutes would be a great answer.*

"Someone from the doctor's office will call you as soon as they have the results. His office information is on the sheet. The storm might delay them a bit," the nurse said. Katie could see the 'don't shoot the messenger' look on her face.

"Don't worry, I know it's not your fault that it's now a waiting game." Katie tried to grace the woman with a slight smile. Again, Katie was glad she wasn't a practitioner of health care, just involved in the paperwork at her workplace.

"More important at the moment, can I run by the drive-thru daiquiri shop and pick up a large margarita on the way home? It might help the wait." Katie tried for a bit of levity and felt like a hopeful puppy.

"Well, I don't think the doctor has a recommendation on that one way or another. I'd join you if I could," said the nurse, retuning Katie's

Weathering the Storm

grin with a quick wink. "Just remember to keep the straw out of the cup until you're in your driveway," she said handing Katie the paperwork to give to the front desk staff.

Katie took the papers and gave the woman a short salute while walking out the door.

It was definitely daiquiri time.

25.8N, 85.0W. 80 MPH. 420 miles southeast of Rienville. Tropical Storm Stella has achieved Hurricane status as a Category 1 storm with sustained winds of 80 miles per hour. NHC/NOAA.

Lola texted "Need a break from Stella?" Pink drinks at my house at 7?' and hit the send button. The message went out to Katie and Rose. Between packing for a possible evacuation, worrying about her Dad and wondering whether to cancel her quilt classes scheduled for next week, she really did need a break. The others probably did as well.

Waiting for her friends to answer, Lola looked at the paper taped to the top of a plastic tub and reviewed the list. The wrought iron rose picture frame her great-grandfather had crafted in his workshop. Her Grandma's quilt with its faded fabrics. Wedding photos. One of the lessons she had learned from her many friends that lost everything in Hurricane Katrina was almost everything is replaceable except the few items that hold a special place in your heart. What went into the tote were those types of things.

Lola noticed Rene had the practical and all-important document box already packed and sitting by the front door. It held the precious insurance policies, mortgage papers, birth certificates, school forms, vet papers and the like. That box had been kept ready since Hurricane Katrina and he was diligent at updating the copies of forms and policies. He could bug out in ten minutes if he had too.

Lola liked living with her treasures and unpacked the tote after each storm scare. Hence the list taped to the top of the box. Forgetting one of these in her hurry to leave would be almost too much to bear. She walked down the hall to start the gathering process. She and Rene were still in limbo concerning their travel plans. The box would soon be filled with her priceless possessions and placed next to Rene's box by the front door.

*

"Pink Drinks at 7??" Katie read the text and immediately felt some tension leave her body.

Weathering the Storm

"Yes!!!" she texted back to Lola. Rose was the resident storm watcher of their group and she could get a good update on Stella from her. Working in a windowless office every day gave Katie a false sense of normalcy.

Formerly Tropical Storm Stella, Hurricane Stella had everyone at work in a tizzy this morning. The office had a storm contingency plan on file and the office manager had enacted it when she arrived at the clinic. Computer backups were in progress and patient appointment lists printed out.

The decision to close the office had been made and everyone would get a piece of the list. They would pick up a phone to call and postpone patient visits. This dentist office would shut down for a minimum of three days. Unfortunately, Katie didn't think it would be paid vacation.

Since moving to Rienville with John, Katie had learned about the nomadic life possible for a member of this community in the fall. Push comes to shove; she'd load up her jeep and head to Nashville as soon as the office officially closed. Seeing her parents was the positive bonus hurricane season could bring.

Not telling her Mom or Dad about her tests would be hard. They were both exceptionally perceptive people and it was weighed on her mind.

She hadn't told anyone about her medical tests. Katie was still waiting for the biopsy results. She figured it would be at least three business days until she heard anything. Hopefully Stella wouldn't arrive in the meantime.

Rose peeked at her cellphone while Mr. and Mrs. Williams discussed the age of the kitchen cabinets. It was the 23rd house she had showed the couple and, as with the others, they had 'issues' with it.

"Pink Drinks at 7?" The text was a lighthouse beacon and Rose, a drowning sailor.

"I don't understand why they would use these handles. They're not cute," said Mrs. Williams as she opened yet another cabinet.

"They obviously like tomatoes," said a slightly perplexed Mr. Williams, looking more closely at the cabinets and the unique hardware.

"Paint and new handles are easy fixes. You can have fun picking out new ones to fit your own style." Rose tried to sound light hearted.

Stepping into the dining room, Rose tapped, "see you then" all in caps and sent it across the airwaves. *7 o'clock cannot come fast enough*. Rose moved toward the kitchen and her critiquing clients.

25.8N, 85.0W. 80 MPH. 420 miles southeast of Rienville.

The three women sat around the blue plastic kiddie pool, occasionally splashing the water with their toes as they sipped on their pink drinks. A slight breeze flitted through the live oaks, gently moving the leaves that were offering much appreciated shade. Above them, clouds in curved rows floated northward. The outer bands of Stella were now evident, though she was days away from paying the Gulf Coast a visit.

It was quiet at the moment. Their get-togethers were not usually categorized by quiet.

Rose wore her sandy brown hair pulled up under a Chicago Cubs baseball cap and sported last year's Mardi Gras krewe t-shirt. She lounged with her head back against the chair and her eyes closed. It had been a long day.

"Stella's either going to be a good girl or a bitch," she said.

"Where do they say she's headed so far," Katie asked. She had barely listened to the weather reports as her mind was on other things.

"It's too early to call but it's still moving toward Pensacola." Rose sighed. "Those poor people." The panhandle of Florida had been hit by two small hurricanes so far this year. Rose knew their tourism season was pretty much shot. Among other things, storms tended to suck all the sand from the beaches and carry it out to sea. She loved those beautiful white beaches.

Lola made swirly patterns in the water with her feet and looked at her friends over the lip of her Mason jar. She smiled at Rose's hat. That Cubs hat had brought Rose and Lola together many years ago. Lola had noticed the hat on the head of the woman in front of her in the long grocery line at Schwegman's. Lola felt called to commiserate over the team's poor season with a kindred spirit. The Cubs had been so bad for so long, only a diehard Cubs fan would be seen in public sporting the iconic logo. With that first conversation, the rest, as they say, was history.

Katie set down her drink in the grass and pulled her long red hair up in a knot at the top of her head. It was still warm for September. She sat in her scrubs from work with the legs rolled up. It had been the dentist office's late day for patients needing work after the usual 4 p.m.

closing time. Whether it was her drink or the comfortable setting, Katie could feel herself starting to relax, a little. It would take a lot of pink drinks to totally forget her current situation.

"Have you decided to leave?" Katie asked, directing the question to both women.

"Too early to call," said Rose, sipping her drink. "If she stays east, we won't have to go. I don't mind leaving, but with the dogs, it's always an adventure." Rose leaned her head back against the lawn chair and looked up into the moving leaves above her head.

"What about you?" the young woman turned to Lola. Katie appreciated having these women in her life. She learned a lot from them, like when to escape from a storm. Around them, she didn't feel so alone. She no longer missed John every day, but he did pop up in her thoughts at times like this.

"I have to convince my Dad to come in off the bayou first. When and if it starts to look really bad, we'll head north. Dad's the lynchpin in the Normandy family evacuation plan." She reached into the cooler for the repurposed orange juice jug and topped off each glass with the sparkly pink liquid. Katie wasn't sure what made its way into the jug. The important thing was it was cold, a little fizzy and definitely yummy.

Katie and Rose both knew Lola's father James. Katie had enjoyed the times she had sat around his picnic table, eating crabs from his traps and listening to his stories.

Some of James' tales were of his exploits surviving Katrina on the bayou. The coonass would not leave his home/camp and almost didn't survive to share his tale. Lola's mother had died the year before the massive storm. James' daughter had shared with her friends that she had suspected James might not have minded so much if the storm had taken him to join his late wife. His grief was still raw during that time. But he and Spot had made it through. It was three days before Lola could get to him and learned he still lived. Three days of hell Lola hoped not to repeat.

The group turned quiet for a few minutes, strains of Jimmy Buffet floating from a neighbor's sound system. Singing of changes of latitudes and attitudes seemed apropos.

Weathering the Storm

"Enough about Stella. Did you hear Mary at our Vet's office has breast cancer?" Rose asked Lola.

Frowning, Lola replied. "No, I hadn't. How bad, do you know? She's only in her 40's I think."

"I don't have many details. She's going to be out for a few months while she has surgery and chemo. Such a shame." Rose glanced over and saw Katie staring down in the pool, a small tear silently falling down her cheek. Rose splashed Lola's leg as she gestured toward their friend. Lola looked over and then passed Rose back a concerned look.

"Katie, do you know Mary? I didn't think you had any pets," Lola quietly asked. The upset woman sitting in front of them seemed foreign to the lively young woman they had come to know.

Katie shook her head and continued to stare at the water in the pool. She wiped the tears with the back of her hand and moved her right foot slowly through the water. Lola gave Rose a 'What now Sherlock?' look. After a few moments, Rose splashed Katie's leg with water to get her attention.

"So, if you don't know Mary, what's on your mind?"

Looking up at her closest friends in Rienville, she straightened her shoulders and swiped at her eyes again before she replied. "I may be in the same boat as Mary."

Stunned, Lola simply stared at the young woman, while Rose pushed aside the dainty straw and took a big slug from her glass. The rustling leaves overhead suddenly sounded very loud in the quiet.

"OK." Lola took a deep breath. "Maybe leaves a lot of wiggle room. So how about you tell us what you know for sure and we'll go from there." Lola tried to sound confident and hoping she had succeeded.

Katie sat quietly, looking down at her feet. Rose grew more concerned. She looked at their young friend, then back to Lola. The two older women had taken to Katie quickly. It was hard to realize they had known each other only a year. With a question in her eye, Rose casually swept a hand in front of her chest and nodded. Lola shrugged and tilted her chin to signal yes.

Rose scooted her chair closer to Katie, threw an arm over her Katie's shoulder and gave it a good squeeze. Making an attempt to put a smile on her face, she quietly started.

"Well Katie-girl, consider yourself lucky. You are in the company of two women who might be uniquely qualified to walk with you through this little adventure. And we have the scars to prove it. Are we talking breast cancer?"

Katie tried to look Rose in the face and failed. Looking down, she watched her feet making swirls in the kiddy pool's tepid water. "It's looking that way". Rose squeezed Katie's shoulders again and tried to get the younger woman to look up at her and Lola.

"My scare turned out to be just that, a bad scare. The lumpectomy removed a tumor that turned out to be benign," said Rose. As Rose started to talk, Katie slowly raised her head and looked at her friend with expressed interest.

"Lola on the other hand, had a mastectomy eleven years ago when she was diagnosed with stage 2 breast cancer."

Katie turned to Lola and glanced briefly at her chest before meeting her gaze. "You've never said anything. Not even when we did that walkathon."

Lola shrugged and tried for a casual response. "I'm not a big fan of pink. Except...," Lola raised her glass to her friends before she took another sip of her drink.

"So now that you know you are in the presence of a virtual fountain of knowledge on this particular problem. Tell us what you know and let's see what we can do to help you." Rose removed her arm from Katie's shoulder, took the young woman's hand in hers and squeezed it. Rose received a small smile in return.

Katie explained the yearly checkup visit, the doctor's concern, the mammogram with the unusual shadow and the biopsy. The relief was palpable; she felt the weight lifted off her shoulders by someone else knowing what was happening.

Weathering the Storm

"OK, we have lots to discuss." Rose poured the rest of the fuchsia liquid into their jars, motioned to Lola with a simple "hey bartender, we're out" wave and passed the jug. Lola was already on her feet to make a new batch.

"Since neither of you will be driving tonight after this next round, I'll let Rene know we will have overnight guests. I'll order pizza. Topping requests?" Lola asked.

"Sausage and mushroom," Rose called out, as Lola turned toward the house. *Might as well have the heartburn kick in.* The alcohol mixed with the added stress in her chest already had her stomach grinding.

"Anything is good," Katie said. She returned her gaze to the swirling water as she sipped her drink.

*

Lola entered the house and went straight to the phone to call Gino's. She placed an order for Rose's favorite with thick crust and a thin crust pepperoni to share with Rene.

As she mixed up a new batch of libations, Rene came in from the bedroom. Their dog Blue followed him into the kitchen.

"Second pitcher in an hour. Somebody's going to be happy," he teased her.

Not looking up, his wife continued to pour and mix. These get-togethers were usually boisterous, verging on frat party loud. As he looked at Rose, Rene's worried expression acknowledged that he could tell something was definitely off tonight.

"Awfully quiet outside." He stood across the kitchen from Lola. "Are they worried about the storm?"

She shook her head and continued to stir.

Rene became concerned. Rose's whole demeanor started warning bells in his head. Two rounds were usually more than enough to last a whole evening for these three. He enjoyed hearing them giggle and they would send him funny looks when he would pass by the den during their winter get-togethers.

"If it's not the storm, what is it?"

"Katie may have breast cancer," Lola mumbled, a quiet tear dropping off her check.

Moving around the kitchen counter, Rene gripped his wife's shoulder. Never expecting that reason, he turned Lola to tuck her up against his chest and held her close.

"It's not confirmed, but it doesn't sound good. She's had the biopsy but can't get the results until this damn storm passes," she said into his chest. Lola tugged on his shirt and tried to burrow in. She would not start bawling. That would not help. Lola always felt more secure standing like this with her husband.

Quietly, he spoke into her hair. "It doesn't mean her experience will be the same as yours." Rene would not wish the hell his wife went through on anyone.

"No, or it could be worse." Her face hidden, she mumbled into his shirt. Rene had learned to decipher her mumbles after more than three decades of marriage.

He looked over her head and out the window toward the small pool at the back of the yard. "And it could be turn out to be like Rose's case," he replied, again squeezing her hard. Rene tried to sound positive while he tried not to think about the dark days after Lola's diagnosis.

After a few moments of listening to Rene's strong and steady heartbeat, she patted his shirt and he released her. She turned on the water tap to cold and splashed her face. While she blinked away the water, he handed her a few paper towels. Lola wiped her face dry.

"Good thing I don't wear make-up." She looked up at him with a hint of a smile.

"Good thing," he said, as he took the used towel out of her hand and gave her a quick kiss.

"Y'all planning a slumber party tonight?" Rene asked as he eyed the pitcher. It would not be the first time the girls had relaxed over their pink drinks to the point of crashing at the house.

Weathering the Storm

"It's looking that way. Pizza should be on its way soon."

"Ok." He headed toward the guest room to get the blankets for the pullout couch in the den. Between the couch and the guest room, Katie and Rose would be comfortable.

Lola turned to the counter and rolled her shoulders before she grabbed the pitcher. She did her best to look more relaxed as she headed back outside.

*

Rose looked out the passenger side window and watched rows of puffy clouds pass over the full moon. Rene was driving her home. *Katie's younger body can be comfortable in a borrowed bed, but I'd rather be in my own bed.* When she decided to call Patrick to pick her up, Rene told her she must be drunk to want to wake her sainted husband at 1 a.m. He said he would drive her home in his truck since he was up anyway. *Rene is not only a good man, but a wise one.* Patrick would have come to get her. However, he would not have been happy that she'd stopped counting the pink drinks hours before.

The three friends had talked about Katie's initial results and focused on positive outcomes. Then the conversation turned to other topics. From deriding the local politicians to fussing about the storm and all it could entail, they talked and laughed and sat silently at times. Comfortable friends in an uncomfortable situation.

The Marino household was not far from Lola & Rene's place; Rienville being only a dozen miles wide. Rose and her driver rode in silence most of the way.

When Rene pulled into the driveway, Rose saw the porch light on, but no doggies in the front window. Rose predicted they would be snuggled with Patrick on the bed. *I'll have to fight for my own pillow since I wasn't there when they all climbed in.*

"Thanks for the ride." Rose groped for the door handle in the dark. She was still having issues with her hand/eye coordination. *Nothing sleep won't cure.*

"It's going to be OK." After watching Rose struggle to open the door, Rene reached over and pulled the handle.

Rose didn't know if he was talking about Stella, Katie's issue or her current inebriation.

"I know," was all she said as she slipped out of the truck. It didn't matter which question she was answering at that moment.

"Thanks again." Rose closed the door and hitched her purse up onto her shoulder. She walked as carefully as possible on the path to her front door.

25.8N, 86.0W. 90 MPH. 379 miles southeast of Rienville.

James sat on the deck and watched the moonlight bounce off the water. Spot lay at his feet, her paws twitching. *Probably chasing squirrels in her personal dreamland.*

As he looked over the bayou, he could see the clouds rolling in waves, just like the tide. He didn't need the Weather Channel to tell him the storm continued to move their way. He could see that by just looking at the sky and the occasional gusts in the breeze. He enjoyed nights like this since the wind kept the temperature down and the mosquitos on the wing.

It was a small gift from Stella.

As he gazed over the railing, James tried to decide what to do after the sun came up. He had battened down all his proverbial hatches and secured anything the wind could take for a ride. There was plenty of water, food and propane. Short of the camp collapsing off its pilings from the winds and surge of a Category 3 storm or better, he was prepared. Stella was just a category 1 hurricane at 90 mph. *A walk in the park in my book, but that didn't mean she can't kick up her heels and make a run for the big time.*

James gently moved the rocker and listened to the swish of the marsh grasses below his home. He had no doubt he and Spot could handle most any contingency. Yet his daughter wanted him off the water and near her for the duration. He could understand her worry. James had given Lola quite a fright during Katrina. It had been rough on Lola when she didn't hear from him for several days. It was tough on him too, knowing she was worried.

Even knowing how distressed Lola was at the thought of James and Spot staying home, he was troubled by the decision to come off the bayou for Stella. His daughter had a comfortable home, but it wasn't the same to him as being in his own place.

And truth be told, he worried about Ms. Beryl. She believed she had no place to go since her family was so far away. He needed to keep an eye on her as well.

There's still time.

James leaned back against the rocker's slats, listening to Spot and the lapping of the water and dozed.

26.1N, 86.6W. 90 MPH. 341 miles southeast of Rienville.

Katie woke up with the soft light of morning coming in the window, thru sunset-colored curtains.

I don't have red curtains, Katie thought as she tried to refocus on the fabric across the room.

Her mouth felt like cotton balls and when she opened her eyes wider, she felt a harsh sensation behind her right eye.

Seeing the bright geometric quilt on the wall beside the bed, her thoughts coalesced. Pink drinks. Delicious, but with a kick. Katie slowly rose to sit on the side of the daybed and took stock. Once Lola's offer of a place to crash in her sewing room was made and accepted, Katie hadn't worried about how many pink drinks she drank and simply enjoyed them. Add the hot pizza to the mix and the knowledge that both Lola and Rose could be sounding boards for the days ahead had helped Katie sleep like a baby.

Not finding a clock on the wall, Katie looked around for her cell phone. She needed to check the time and hadn't replaced her watch since it broke. Luckily it was sitting on her purse next to the daybed. 7:43 flashed across the screen when she hit the power button. It was a good thing she wasn't expected into work.

Time to get up and out of Lola's hair. It wasn't the first time she had stayed over in the sewing room after a late-night visit with her friends and a cocktail or two or three. After she slipped on her shoes and tried to rub out some of the wrinkles from her scrubs, she opened the door and headed down the hall to the bathroom. From experience, she knew Lola kept guest necessities like new toothbrushes and fresh towels in the cabinet above the sink. She finished washing up and felt more human. Katie returned to the guest room and she quickly made the bed. Grabbing her purse, Katie went to find her hostess. *Time to face the day and all its wonders.*

26.2N, 86.1W. 90 MPH. 356 miles southeast of Rienville.

"Stay or go?"

Rene has always been a man of few words. Lola took down the wind chimes from the tree in the backyard.

As she and the girls sat under this tree last night digesting Katie's news, she had heard their tinkling sounds wafting through the trees. Since she had concentrated primarily on organizing the inside of the house for a possible evacuation, she had put off the outside.

It was amazing to her how much stuff people collected outside. Truth be told, not just people, but her and Rene. Lawn chairs, grills, smoker, four birdfeeders, three wind chimes, a garden flag, three kayaks and more.

The chimes made a great clanking noise when they folded onto themselves as Lola put them in the bin. It had to be done. Winds of any speed from an approaching storm, even a small one like Stella was at the moment, could send a plastic birdfeeder crashing into a window.

"Don't know yet," Lola answered as she reached for another set of chimes. This one was made of bent silverware; old fashioned forks and spoons. She had looked at the vendor's chimes year after year at the local craft fair. She always enjoyed their tinkling chorus as she walked through the booths. At a fair ten years ago, she had decided she wanted to enjoy that sound more than once a year and bought this set on the spot.

Remembering last night's conversation, she looked at the twisted forks and thought it funny how some people found a cancer diagnosis muddled their thinking. When it was Lola who heard the news, she found it suddenly made many decisions painfully clear. Enjoy the sweet things now. Listen to the chimes today.

Rene reached up to take a wooden feeder down from a tall shepherd's crook. It was empty at the moment anyway. As it was fall, there was plenty for the birds to eat sitting around the yard and Rene had not been prompt when it needed to be refilled.

Stella had stalled like a mule not wanting to cross a creek. She sat out in the Gulf, churning up the surf and people's anxieties. She could build up speed and come crashing through their town fast and rough.

Or she could meander through in low gear. Outsiders thought people would like that type of hurricane better. But the truth was, a slow-moving Category 1 hurricane could cause a lot more problems than a fast-moving Cat 3. It all came down to the water. A stalled storm had a tendency to push water from the Gulf up into the lakes, rivers and bayous. When the rains inevitably came on the back end of the storm, there would be no place for the runoff to go. If that was the case, their backyard would be Lake Normandy for days.

Envisioning the backyard with more water than grass, Lola had to smile. *The dogs would love it if we stayed.*

"Stella has slowed down to creeping speed and is still at 90 miles per hour last time I checked." Lola picked up a dog toy from the grass. "The next update is in about an hour." She tossed the toy into the bin.

Rene surveyed the backyard. He needed to make room for the big items in the garage. It would be a tight fit considering there was already a lawn mower, his four-wheeler and the souped-up shopping carts waiting to be decorated for next year's Mardi Gras parade. It could be done. *We just need to clear a path to the beer fridge for as long as the power lasts.* He would station a large cooler by the frig. When the power went out, he could pop the bags of ice from the freezer into a cooler, along with the beer and drinks. That would be part of the shelter in place plan.

Such was the quandary each time a storm formed. Stay or go.

Rienville was east of the Big Easy, which made evacuating a little easier for locals. The general population in New Orleans tended to head toward Baton Rouge, or if things got really bad, Houston. Those tough-nosed Texans were whispered about at crawfish boils until the time came when Louisianans needed the proverbial port in a storm.

"Should I guess which way James is leaning?" Rene tugged the Sheppard's crook out of the ground.

"What do you think?" Lola snorted. She knew snorting wasn't the best look for her. However, it fit the question. So far, James wasn't leaving the bayou. There wasn't even any real discussion at this point.

"Well, if she comes in low and slow, he'll be fine."

Weathering the Storm

That was true. Rising water was no problem for James' home. He would only have issues if the surge got above twenty-two feet or if the winds got past a hundred miles per hour. He had built the modified camp to withstand a lot of what nature could offer. James had made it clear to everyone that it was the last home he planned to own.

Lola's mom had died only eight years into their retirement and James couldn't stand to stay in their longtime home without her. He updated the family camp he had built on Bayou Oiseaux and moved there with Spot for the peace and quiet. Over the years, Lola had witnessed the healing power of the peaceful bayou on her father. Lola also suspected he'd found a bit of 'lagniappe', a little something extra special, in the form of his friendship with his neighbor, Ms. Beryl.

"The paper bin's ready." Rene lifted a kayak off the rack and started to walk toward the gate in the fence.

Looking around the backyard, Lola checked off several items on her storm readiness to do list and followed him to the garage. Still the question was there. *Pack up and head out or hunker down. Always the big question.*

26.2N, 86.7W. 90 MPH. 336 miles southeast of Rienville.

It was still early as Rose sat in her flannel pajamas in her home office, nursing a cup of her favorite red tea. Her white mug, with a mountain logo and the phrase, 'The first person to make a mountain out of molehill was a Real Estate Agent' said it all. As she looked at her computer screen, Rose reviewed the list of properties she managed and mentally checked off the ones whose owners still needed to be called. The home would need to be secured and weather-proofed.

Almost everything had been taken care of. After the past few years, Rose's clients knew the drill. Things had changed since Hurricane Katrina, when she didn't have a written storm plan for the clients who used her to manage their rental properties. Not only did Rose spend hours getting her own roof repaired, she grew very frustrated handling the repairs and gutting crews for properties where she couldn't reach the owners.

What a pain that was. She blew on her tea and took a sip. Now, all her clients knew they were responsible for their own storm remediation from day one. If she did not leave town and after this storm passed, Rose would do a courtesy check on the properties. Otherwise, her owners were on their own. Written waivers were wonderful things.

As she looked around her office, Rose took comfort in little sayings posted on her bulletin board and the photos around the computer screen. Hurricanes always made her think about her stuff. Although she had learned she could live without it, Rose also recalled how precious some things could be.

Sitting back in her old, yet comfortable office chair, she looked out the window and thought of Katie. Rose's stomach trembled slightly thinking of the fear Katie must have felt when she got her preliminary results.

Rose smiled at the memory of her mother Anne's determination to get her initial diagnosis confirmed and treatment plans underway ASAP. Patrick had been a calming influence during that time when Rose's brain couldn't land on a single thought for more than a moment. On the flip side, Anne had been a cross between a bulldog and a Marine gunnery sergeant. Anne was going to get answers and get them now.

Weathering the Storm

They were both just what Rose had needed at the time. The realtor couldn't imagine Katie handling this by herself. It seemed an unnecessary burden. As she reached for her cell phone, Rose decided what Katie needed was a bulldog.

*

Katie still didn't know if she needed to leave or could safely stay. Stella was stationary in the Gulf, whatever that meant, and everyone's plans seemed to be on hold. And people were tense.

In truth, she hadn't paid much attention to all the hype in the media about 'getting a game plan' and put together a hurricane preparedness kit. She had assumed she would leave if it looked bad.

You know what they say about when you assume something. She looked around her small kitchen. There was no bottled water, weather radio or much in the way of food. Just a few cans of Blue Runner red beans. She grimaced at the thought of eating them cold out of the can if the power went out.

I am in no way prepared for staying through a storm.

A small sense of dread came over her as Katie came to the conclusion a trip to Walmart was in order. Katie's shoulder's bunched as she walked to the front door. *Walmart and the interesting people who congregate there: evacuation looks better and better.*

Grabbing her keys to her older model, green Jeep, Katie locked the front door and made her way to the car. She looked at the front of the house and made a mental note to take down the American flag from the side of the house. Although she had lived in the little shotgun rental house for almost a year, she hadn't done much to decorate the yard. *All the better with a storm possibly heading this way. Less to put in the storage shed.*

Making her way down 5th Street, traffic was slightly heavier than for a regular Rienville afternoon.

"I guess a lot of people are still on the fence about leaving," she mumbled to herself as she entered the Racetrack station. With most of the pumps occupied, Katie found an empty pump on the end and decided to fill up the tank. *Just in case the road calls.*

Taking her insulated to-go cup inside, Katie filled it partly with the crushed ice she preferred and the rest of the way with her favorite soft drink. As she waited in line to pay, she scanned the other customers for familiar faces. For a change, she recognized no one. Thinking on that, she was often amazed at how many people she had met in Rienville since she had arrived. It was not unusual for her to receive a friendly 'good morning' from an acquaintance when she picked up her favorite travel mug each morning on the way to work.

Heeding the call for 'next guest', Katie walked toward the counter and ordered $20 on pump sixteen and a quick pick Powerball ticket from Kyle, one of the managers who was pulling cashier duty during the rush.

"There you go Darlin'," Kyle said as he smiled at Katie. She traded the bills needed to cover her purchases for the lottery ticket.

"Thanks. This storm is keeping you guys busy?" She didn't feel bad chatting a bit since the line had temporarily dwindled down to her and the customer talking with another cashier.

"We're doing OK. This isn't our first rodeo, you know." Kyle gave Katie a big grin as he leaned on the register.

"Well, it is mine. What do you think? Do I stay or should I go?" Getting a consensus from locals couldn't hurt.

"That's a tough call. Before Katrina, we'd never leave. Now, we are ready to move if they say move. The wife has everything ready if they shut us down. Which way would you head?"

"I can go visit my parents in Nashville." Katie received her receipt from him and tucked it into her wallet. "I just don't know what to do." She shrugged as she put her purse strap over her shoulder.

"We have a little time yet. Stella is a finicky little witch right now. When she starts on the rest of her trip north, just watch her carefully and listen to the people on the radio. Trust your gut and you'll know

Weathering the Storm

what to do," said Kyle, looking behind Katie at the new customers coming down the aisle.

"Thanks for the advice and take care." Katie moved toward the exit.

"You too Darlin'. Next guest?" Kyle motioned the next person in line forward.

Katie tooled down the road and sang loudly along with one of her favorite Lady Antebellum songs. She was headed toward the local big box store. As she sipped her drink, Katie worked on a mental shopping list of basics that could get her through a few days without power.

The shopping center parking lot was busy. Katie ended up nearer the garden center than her usual entrance. She nodded to the elderly store greeter in his U.S. Army veteran hat and grabbed a shopping cart.

As always, Katie found shopping at Wal-Mart kin to attending a three-act play. Her friend Darrell might call it performance art, for all the drama happening between shoppers. *How can people shop in their pajamas?* She passed two twenty-somethings in tank tops, flannel bottoms and flip flops. *They looked like they just rolled out of bed.* She could not imagine going out in public in the clothes she slept in, as she walked past the pair and headed down the aisle toward the bottled water display.

She tried to remember the notes she read on the state's emergency website. Katie grabbed six gallons of purified water and a twelve pack of diet sodas. No one would want to weather a storm with her if she didn't get her caffeine fix. As she strolled down the aisles, she grabbed a box of strawberry pop-tarts, a loaf of bread, a bag of apples, a few bananas. Put that together with the peanut butter and jelly, a few other items and a couple of bags of ice, she'd survive. Katie started to feel a bit better about her plan of action, such as it was.

Noticing a big display, Katie grabbed a bag of self-starting charcoal and tossed it into her basket. She could heat up the frozen soup from the freezer and her favorite red beans on her little charcoal grill on the deck if needs must.

Moving toward the check-out stands, Katie saw a familiar face. Mary from her Sunday school class and her daughter were pushing a large cart loaded with the makings for a big party.

"How goes it Katie?" Mary's daughter veered off to look at the end of the season clearance clothing rack when her Mom hailed the other shopper.

"I think OK. It looks like you're staying?" Katie smiled as she perused the chips, beer and cookies in the basket. *Maybe Mary's house was the place to be in a hurricane.*

"Probably. If they decide the storm will make landfall near here, Randy will be on duty at the hospital for the duration. If it's a Category 2 or under, we'll stay close to him. It can be pretty miserable with the heat, but we make it a staycation for the kids. I let them stay up late and we eat stuff we don't normally have in the house. We can always cool off in the pool." Mary kept an eye on her daughter while leaning on the shopping basket. Mary's husband was in charge of the physical plant at the hospital.

"Aren't you afraid of falling trees hurting someone?" Katie had heard that a lot of damage in any storm came from the beautifully tall longleaf pines falling and slicing through house roofs like butter.

"We only have a few pines in the back of the yard and mostly hardwoods around the house." "The oaks are pretty sturdy. I don't worry about them."

Katie looked puzzled as she noticed several plastic containers of baby wipes in her friend's basket. Mary followed her look down and laughed. Katie raised an eyebrow and gave her friend a quizzical look.

"No babies on the way at the Guidry house." Mary laughed. "The look on your face is priceless." The youngest Guidry was the teenager slowly looking through the t-shirts across the aisle. "Baby wipes are great for using to clean up after being outside. Saves water and make your skin feel cooler. Get yourself a pack and make sure you get the ones with aloe. They don't dry out your skin."

Weathering the Storm

"Thanks for the clarification." Katie grinned. "Any other useful tips for a first-time storm rookie?"

"If you decide to stay, fill up your bathtub with water. You can use it to flush your toilets if you lose power. Have at least one good flashlight with extra batteries and make sure you have a car charger that works with your phone." Mary had delivered her list of instructions like a drill sergeant.

"Been through a storm or two, huh?" Katie was turning her cart toward the flashlight aisle.

"Or two. Rachel, come on. We need to get going." Mary turned toward the front of the store.

"Take care Mary. I'll see you next week at church."

"Let's hope," she said as she started to move down the aisle. Mary stopped and looked back. "Hey Katie."

Turning back, she looked toward her friend. "Yeah?"

"One more thing." The look she gave Katie brokered no humor. "If they tell you to leave, leave. There's nothing here you can't live without." Mary used something other than her usual cheery tone.

"Got it. Be safe." Katie turned back to her cart and continued toward the flashlights.

*

Rose called Dr. Hilliard MacDermitt on Saturday. She had waited until it was a reasonable hour. Not too early, but before his day could really get going. Rose didn't have a problem bothering him at home on a weekend. She was one of those unique people who understood that sometimes the formalities would have to be ignored to get the job done. This doctor did too.

If it had been a weekday, she would have sat in his office waiting room until he could give her a few minutes of his time between patients.

41

For years, they had shared a love of all things Mardi Gras as well as the fight against cancer; her battle from the personal side. He was one of her knights in shining armor. Several years back, while they lingered after one of their krewe's board meetings, Hill learned of Rose's cancer fight. He'd shared his plans to enhance treatment options and support services locally so women, and the occasional man, would not have to run to Houston to have a shot at beating breast cancer. Rose became one of his biggest advocates and a relentless worker bee for raising funds.

On the second ring, MacDermitt, esteemed oncologist and a man not afraid to dress up as a chicken for a good cause, answered his cell phone.

"Hey Rosie girl. If you are calling to talk us out of our theme again, it won't work. Carol is set on wearing the wench outfit in plaid this year." The entire MacDermitt family was gearing up to represent their medieval Scottish ancestors in the krewe's upcoming Mardi Gras parade. With his dark red hair and ruddy coloring, put a kilt on Dr. MacDermitt and he'd look like he'd just jumped off the cover of a tawdry romance novel. She and Carol had laughed about it, and made teasing comments about the kilt, for weeks.

"No, we're good. Patrick doesn't have the knees for a kilt anyway." The two friends chatted for a few moments about parade plans before Rose got down to the serious business.

"I've got a little problem at the moment and I hope you can help."

The noise behind the physician became quieter as he moved away from where the kids ran around laughing and the dog barked. Rose knew the doctor to have a big heart and he would understand she would not have called on a Saturday morning, and with a storm in the Gulf, without a good reason.

"Go ahead. What's the problem?"

"My friend Katie had an unusual mammogram and it was recommended that she have a needle biopsy. She had it done last week. Katie hasn't received the biopsy results and the doctor she's seeing has already closed his office for the duration due to our alleged impending visit from Stella."

Weathering the Storm

"Who's the physician?"

Rose named a prominent doctor with offices on both sides of Lake Pontchartrain. She heard an exasperated grunt over the phone. Rose had heard rumors on the hospital grapevine about the pathologist in questions. What she believed, and what Hilliard was too nice to mention, was that along with two offices, the doctor in question had a wife on one side of the lake and a close personal acquaintance on the other. Rose's theory was he probably used the storm as an excuse to visit his cabin in the mountains with one without the knowledge of the other.

"Did she have her tests at Rienville General?"

"Yes, she did." Rose provided more details about Katie's situation. Twenty-five years old, single, alone in town and scared. Rose particularly understood the scared part. So, did he. Hilliard was a good doctor.

"Is there any way she can get those results sooner rather than later? I would think they should be ready and are probably sitting in someone's e-mail." Rose tried not to sound as frustrated as she felt.

"I'll see what I can find out through the pathology department. Have her call my office at 7:30 on Monday morning. Give her the inside office line number. We've scaled down the patient schedule, but we're not closing yet. I'll do my best to get her some kind of answer."

Hilliard MacDermitt was one many local doctors who stayed at the hospital during storms. Once he got Carol and the kids on their way to Memphis for a visit with her folks, Hilliard bunked in his office in the medical building when he wasn't on duty. A few of his staff were also emergency on-call personnel. They would see patients for their regular appointments until an evacuation order came. Then those staying would shift from the office wing to the hospital proper and do what needed to be done.

"You're a good man, Charlie Brown." Rose moved her antiquated, but highly valuable, Rolodex to the "M" section and confirmed the semi-secret phone number. Rose knew she was not the only person in town with it and understood what a precious commodity it was.

"No problem. I'm making myself a note now to let Margie know the call will be coming in."

"And for this my friend, I might have to find a group of bagpipers to march in front of your merry band in the parade." Rose had attempted the promise in a Celtic accent with little success.

She could hear him grin when he answered, "Aye, ye be a good lass," with a heavy dose of brogue.

As she signed off, Rose thought her Saturday was starting out a lot sunnier than the weather forecast. She tapped in Katie's number to relay the news with a lighter heart.

*

Katie was putting away her storm prep purchases when the phone rang. Digging into her shorts pocket for her cellphone, she recognized the number when she looked at the screen.

"Hey Rose. What's the latest news on Stella?"

"She's still sitting and spinning like a drunk blond on a bar stool. Not doing nothing but causing a scene."

Katie smiled. *When a storm causes this much angst, you might as well have fun with it.*

"Do you have these sayings written down somewhere?" Katie laughed as she placed the new candles onto the kitchen counter, next to the flashlight batteries. There is no use putting things away since it would be too dark to find them if the power went out.

"No. They just pop out, but maybe I should. Could write a book and make a million." Then Rose got down to business. "Did your landlord leave you any sandbags?"

"I haven't seen any. There are some little piles of sand in the backyard. Not enough to put in a bag."

"OK, then we need to get you some today. What does your schedule look like?"

Weathering the Storm

Katie looked around her cherry-themed kitchen. "I think I have things covered here. I just have to bring in the lawn chairs from the patio and a few other items. That will take five minutes. I'm hoping if I leave them out, this will all blow over and I won't need to."

"Not going to happen," Rose said with a little excitement in her voice. As much as she hated hurricanes and what they could do to her town and her business, they did bring a little something different to her life, a change of pace. A hot, stressful, sweaty change, but a change none the less.

"You can leave those things out for a while longer. Even if Stella comes in with just tropical storm winds, you don't want things flying into your windows. You do need a few sandbags just in case the catch basins get clogged."

Katie had learned over the past few months from her neighbors that catch basins, or storm drains from where she grew up, were crucial to getting water out of the low-lying neighborhoods and away from houses. One or two basins clogged with grass clippings, pine needles or trash could back up water into yards and homes fast. She had witnessed it during a heavy spring rain one evening. One of her neighbors had stood by with a rake keeping a drain down the street clear for an hour in the downpour when the water started rising up and down the street.

"You only need about a dozen bags for your front and back doors. They are heavy so I'll borrow Patrick's truck. I'll bring the shovel." Rose was already planning the trip to the sand pile.

"Shovel? I thought you just drove up to the parish maintenance barn and they load them up in the truck?" Katie had read in the newspaper that the local government used trustee labor from the parish jail to operate automated sandbag filling stations at three locations in the parish.

"That's one way to get them. I think you need to have the whole experience for your first storm. Plus, I already heard the lines are pretty long down the service road and backed up onto the interstate. We'll go to the old levee board building. They always dump a truck-load of sand and a pile of bags there for people in the outlying areas. If you have work gloves, bring them. If not, that's fine. I'll pick you up in 30." Rose rang off before Katie could ask any more questions.

Katie didn't have any gloves except for her winter gloves from Tennessee. She was pretty sure that's not what Rose meant. She did think it sounded like dirty work, so she went down her short hallway to her bedroom. After she changed clothes, she looked at her shoes. Rose had mentioned a shovel and she knew shovels and flip flops do not mix. She looked further back into her closet and found her scuffed, brown hiking boots. Grabbing a pair of socks from the dresser, she walked back to the living room, sat on the couch and put them on.

The boots brought back memories of the last time she had worn them. She and John had gone camping in the Ozarks a few months before his transfer came in. They had acted like the kids, splashing through streams and climbing onto rock ledges to get the best views of the lake in the valley. It had been a wonderful time and she was thankful for the memories. As she thought of the fun they had on that trip, a bit of the sadness over the hard times that followed filled her. It would be a long time, she thought, before his leaving would not bring back some of the sadness. Then she reminded herself the choice to stay in Rienville had been hers to make.

Katie straightened her shoulders and gave herself a shake. She got up from the couch before she'd start tearing up. *Wallowing is not productive.* She had told herself this on many occasions. Keeping busy was the key.

While she waited for Rose, the young woman ventured outside into the muggy air. She walked to the storage shed to grab the big red cooler and bring it back to the kitchen. She'd keep the bags of ice in the freezer.

Check off one more item on the to-do list.

26.7N, 87.9W. 95 MPH. 269 miles southeast or Rienville.

Rose drove toward Katie's street in Patrick's ancient blue Ford. The radio in the truck was belting out a Donna Summer number from her high school days. Since all Patrick listened to was country music and talk radio, he probably didn't even know she had the last button on the console programmed to the old 70's station. He either didn't know or he humored her by letting it stay. *God knows, he never listens to it himself.*

The truck had served her husband and family well. It had been the first new vehicle Patrick had purchased, buying it a few years before they were married. It still ran well, dents and faded seats and all. It regularly hauled 50-pound bags of dog food, furniture for when the kids moved, and it was still their Friday night date ride.

Despite the heat and humidity, Rose drove with the windows down. The better to belt out, at full volume, the back-up lyrics for Donna. Today, the truck was on sandbag duty and not for the first time.

As she drove through the neighborhood, things looked relatively normal on the surface. Kids rode bikes past her on their way to the park; dogs barked as they ran along fence lines. If you didn't know better, all looked well. Upon closer inspection, Rose noticed what was missing. Things like lawn chairs, garden flags and hanging flower baskets. They were put up until the storm passed. The only ornamentation left in the yards were the bright pink blossoms on the crepe myrtles and the cherry colored geraniums in people's cement planters.

Rose tooted the horn as she pulled into Katie's driveway and looked toward the front door. Katie leaned out the doorway and waved, then disappeared back into the house. While Rose sang about September with Earth, Wind and Fire, Katie came out of the house. Hitching the screen door with her hip, she locked the door and headed down the walk.

Dressed in an old canoe trip t-shirt, denim peddle-pushers, a bright blue and orange ball cap and her hiking boots, she was ready to move dirt, sand or whatever needed to be done.

"Hey," she said as she climbed into the passenger seat. Rose was happy to see a smile on her face.

"Ready to make some sandbags?" Rose put the truck in gear and backed out of the drive.

"I guess. I've never needed any before. Not much call for them where I used to live."

"I'm afraid this is kind of a yearly activity. Unfortunately, the bags they pass out fall apart after a few months or we could reuse them," Rose turned down the road and headed toward the levee building.

"They are just some extra protection. When the water starts rising in your yard, you'll be happy to have a few extra inches blocking the doors since your place is on a slab." They listened to a lively disco tune from some now defunct hair band.

As she pulled onto the gravel drive for the municipal building, Rose glanced at Katie's profile for a moment before stopping just inside the gate. It was time to bring up the elephant lounging on the console between them.

"Katie, I hope it's OK. I called a friend of mine about your test results." Rose waited for her young friend's response, not sure what to expect for her meddling. Although Rose had not known Katie long, she hoped it was long enough for this type of intrusion into the younger woman's life

"Thanks for trying to help, but I don't know really what you can do. The doctor has closed his office until the storm passes." Katie pushed back the hair that had come loose from her ponytail while they drove with the windows open.

"He's an oncologist at the hospital and I called him this morning. He said if your biopsy was done at the hospital, he can access the results with your permission and give you an opinion."

"Can he really?" Katie was awed by Rose's actions. She knew her friend had connections in Rienville but had not thought to ask for her to put them in action for her benefit.

"Well, it will be sort of a second opinion before getting the first. At least you would know something either way and a lot sooner." Rose put the truck back into gear and continued down the long gravel road.

Weathering the Storm

Sitting quietly, Katie thanked God for such a wonderful, meddling friend. Turning with a grin on her face, she beamed at Rose. "I'd be grateful to know something sooner rather than later. What do I need to do?" She was ready to make the call that minute. Rose moved toward a large pile of sand with a line of parked vehicles in front of it.

"Before I drop you off at home, I'll give you Hill's, Dr. Hillard MacDermitt's, number. You're to call his office on Monday before office hours start. His receptionist Margie will be watching for your call."

"Thank you Rose." Katie squeezed her friend's arm and felt her eyes tearing up. Rose slowed down to park.

"Anytime Chickadee," Rose said with a wink.

Looking out the windshield, Katie saw what looked like a giant sandbox. Framed on three sides by cement blocks and wooden planks, the pile of sand was enormous. The adults working there looked like kids playing in the dunes at the beach. A few people had their cars backed up to the pile, filling bags from a stack of white sacks sitting off to the side on the ground. A few people had shovels. One mom with two young kids had the children using to-go cups to fill a bag. Most of their sand returned to the pile at their feet rather than entering the receptacle. The kids giggled and tried another cupful.

After they got out of the truck, Rose dropped the tailgate and pulled out a shovel. She pointed to the pile of empty bags and told Katie to start with a dozen. The sand was dry on top of the pile but dampened toward the bottom. They'd start with the lighter, drier sand. No use in making more work for themselves, Rose told her friend.

They began to fill sandbags, taking turns with one shoveling and the other trying the bag shut with the attached cord and lifting it into the truck bed. Thinking about her days of lying by the beach with her toes in the white sand, she'd never had guessed the bags would be so heavy.

After a half dozen, Katie stopped to wipe the sweat from her forehead, pulling the neckline of her t-shirt up and over her face. The breeze helped to keep the air cooler, but the temperature was still in the high 80's and the wind brought humidity with it.

Reaching down to tie the latest bag, a shadow fell at her feet.

"Nice hat," said the shadow. "Let me give you a hand with that." The voice spoke quietly with just a hint of the local accent.

Realizing he was talking about her University of Tennessee at Martin hat, Katie looked up to see a slightly crooked smile come from beneath a faded orange baseball cap with what looked like chew marks on the bill. A smudged white University of Tennessee at Knoxville logo was sewn on the front.

"Okay, thanks," she said as he tossed the sandbag up into the ones already in the truck bed. Katie had noticed him help load some bags for a group of older ladies when Rose first drove up. Katie thought he was with them. When they drove off, he was still standing by the sand pile.

"If you ladies fill 'em up, I'd be happy to load them for you." The smile was still directed at Katie as he nodded in Rose's direction.

"Best deal I've heard all day." Rose said as she handed Katie another bag. Rose stuck out her gloved hand as she introduced herself.

"Rose Marino." She gave the man a quick shake, "and this is my friend Katie Woodruff."

The man extended his hand to Katie after releasing Rose's. "Jake Mesch." He gave her a firm handshake.

"Mesch. Any relation to Jamie Mesch?" Rose eyed him more closely. From prior experience, Katie knew this could become a deep conversation of local family trees and took the opportunity to take a break. As she leaned on the shovel, Katie could feel the sweat slide down her back.

"My uncle." Jake used a bandana to wipe the back of his neck before putting it into the back pocket of his cargo pants.

"Makes sense now why you look familiar. Sold Jamie and Cindy their first house years ago. Which one of Jamie's brothers is your Daddy?" Rose worked to get a bag ready to be filled. Katie was always amazed at her friend's interconnections in Rienville.

Weathering the Storm

"Jean." He was happy to take a break for a minute.

Rose nudged Katie and then bent over to fill the spade with sand. "I went to school with the Mesch brothers. Poor Mrs. Mesch bless her heart. Four boys in almost as many years and she had her hands full. All of them were named after Catholic saints starting with the letter 'J'." She winked toward Jake when she added, "and each one more handsome than the next."

"I'll share that last bit the next time I see them," he grinned as he picked up another filled bag.

"No need to do that. They all knew the girls adored them back in the day. I remember Jean heading north after school, but I couldn't remember where. Is your hat a good clue?" Rose gestured toward his head.

"Yes ma'am, it is. Dad went to UT and met Mom. She's from a small town outside of Oak Ridge and after he got his engineering degree, they moved close to her family."

"Are you a UT grad too?" asked Rose.

"The hat's my Dad's. I only went for a year. Sitting in a classroom for another three years wasn't for me. I went and got my certification in HVAC systems and I worked in Oak Ridge for a while."

"Oak Ridge is a long drive from Rienville. What has you down here with a storm coming?" Katie tried not to sound too curious even if she was. Any mention of Tennessee made Katie feel a bit closer to home.

"A day's drive is not too far really. Last year, the family decided Mawmaw shouldn't live alone anymore and she didn't want to move out of her home. I was looking for a change and decided I'd give it a shot at being her roommate for a while." Jake grinned at them both. "I can work anywhere, and the house is big enough that I can keep an eye on her and we both still have our own space."

"Takes care of his Mawmaw can fix an air conditioner and has the Mesch good looks. I'd have to say you're golden, Jake." Rose watched

Jake's neck turn a pretty shade of carmine as his face brightened with a cute grin when he glanced in Katie's direction.

"What do you think Katie?" Rose bumped her friend's shoulder. Her teasing had caused Katie to sport a matching flush.

"I think we need to get back to filling bags so we can move out of the way for the next wave of people." Katie quickly picked up the bag she had dropped and crouched down to hold it for Rose and her shovel. Her eyes focused on the empty bag.

"All righty then, back to work." Rose spoke casually as she filled the bag, "This is Katie's first taste of hurricane season fun." Katie tied the bag and Jake hauled it to the truck.

"It's not so bad really. Just be prepared for no electricity for a few days and if they say leave, listen to them." He turned back from the rear of the truck.

"That's what I'm trying to do. Rose has given me some tips on what I need, and I followed some of the suggestions from the newspaper. Are you ready?" she asked him with genuine interest.

"Mawmaw has never liked to leave so she's got the house pretty much stocked. Katrina was the only time she left. She thinks it got so bad then partly because she wasn't here to pray it away."

Further conversation was put aside. The sound of the 'shush' of shovels into the pile and the slide of the sand into bags continued. From the nearby woods, the cicadas sang their song, hitting a crescendo and then receding.

In a few minutes, they had what they needed finished and Rose closed the tailgate.

She stored the shovel alongside the sandbags and pulled two bottles of water out of the cooler sitting behind her seat. She passed one to Katie and the other to Jake and then grabbed one for herself. She relished the cold as the water flowed down her throat. Rose peeked at her co-workers, as she rubbed the cool plastic over her forehead. Even after this short bit of manual labor, the three looked like a pile of damp dishrags. After a few moments, Rose tossed the empty bottle behind her seat and she motioned for the others to do the same.

Weathering the Storm

Rose held out her hand to Jake. When he took it, she pulled him into a quick hug.

"Appreciate the help. Hope you all make it through the storm alright." She released him. Katie stood on the passenger side of the truck with the door open, ready to get in.

"I'm sure we'll be fine. Mawmaw's house is raised and she's never had a problem with flooding, even in Katrina. A couple of my cousins will come stay with us if it gets bad since their homes are on the water. Hold on a second." He trotted off to his truck, a restored Ford Bronco with a magnetic business sign attached to the driver's door. Leaning in the window for something on the visor, he walked back and gave each woman a business card sporting the Mesch AC logo on it.

"Still working on my marketing here. Keep me in mind if you need help after the storm."

Rose thanked him for the card, as did Katie, and climbed in the truck. After closing the door, Jake stood next to the passenger window with a hand on the side mirror. His hazel eyes looked bright while perusing the inside of the classic truck, as well as the woman in the passenger seat.

"Don't let the storm worry you. If you need any help getting your place secure, let me know. The number on the card is my cell." As Katie nodded her thanks, Jake patted the mirror and then stepped back as Rose turned over the ancient engine. With a quick wave, she put it in gear and drove off.

As she looked in the rear-view mirror, Rose began to hum 'You Are My Sunshine' while Katie turned the card over in her hand. Thoughts of a helpful man with pretty eyes under a UT hat made her smile and soon she was humming along.

*

Lola half listened to the Cubs game on the satellite radio station as she drove toward her dad's camp. Deciding it was another losing effort in yet another losing year, she cut off the announcer in mid-sentence. As a diehard Cubs fan since before their marriage, Lola felt entitled to turn off an occasional game without remorse. She had endured enough unexciting games over the years and had earned the right.

Shoulder high marsh grass waved in the wind on both sides of the highway. She tried to concentrate on her driving while also working on her list of reasons James should head inland should Stella get cranked up. Every so many yards, a break in the grass would show a patch of water sporting that odd green-blue color found in the swamp. Further down the road, a snowy egret picked its way through the tall grass, looking for its next meal.

Usually Lola looked forward to driving down this road. There was little traffic and no billboards. She mostly saw tall, dusty green grass, blue sky with puffy cotton clouds, and birds skimming over the water. Passing over a bridge, she noted there were quite a few cars parked in the swamp tour's lot. It was a good thing they still had customers. It was hard on the small businesses when they had to shut down indefinitely due to these types of storms. They needed to get the money in while they could.

Back to the case at hand. Lola continued down the highway. Situations like this were some of the times she missed her mom the most. If Audrey were still alive, she would not have to make this drive. Audrey liked a good adventure, but also had a good head on her shoulders. A little inconvenience in the way of no AC and cooking on the gas grill for a few days would not faze her. She had ridden out a few minor storms with James at their home in town. But when the word came from the powers that be to get out of Dodge, Audrey had been ready and on the road without looking back. Their home had been on what she liked to refer to as 'the ridge', a mere two feet above the rest of the subdivision. Those two feet had saved them from flooding when their neighbors had taken water and their home became a port in the storm for many during difficult times. Her Mom always said better to be out of harm's way during the worst of it and able to come back ready to help those who would need it.

Weathering the Storm

James had been the head of the Coubillion household, but it was Lola's mother who was the captain who handled the day to day operations. When she said it was time to evacuate, he loaded up the car with the boxes she had packed, and they hit the road. After she had passed and James moved to the camp on Bayou Oiseaux, storms had a different feel for Lola.

As she turned right off the highway onto Cypress Road, Lola drove past several gravel driveways veering off the main road before turning onto the last one on the right. A hand painted sign saying Serenity Hill II was nailed to a tree close to the road. Serenity Hill was what mom had named their home on the ridge. When they built the camp, she saw it as their own home away from home.

Lola parked next to her father's truck. She got out and picked up the picnic basket from the floorboard. Inside was stew made from some of the last of the venison in the chest freezer and pumpkin muffins. Smiling, she walked up the steps, as the wind blew her silver hair around the reading glasses she used as a makeshift headband. It was always a personal triumph for her when her plan to have a near empty freezer at the start of storm season came to fruition. Although, this year, she still had more than a cooler's worth left.

The camp was quiet when she reached the top of the stairs. A note was written on the chalkboard next to his front door. "Down a ways. Be back by 1". The board had been Audrey's idea. Since she claimed James never paid attention when she said she was running an errand or such, Audrey put up the board and left her husband notes. *It's funny and a little sad that now he leaves notes almost to himself.* Lola was glad that burglars weren't common around the bayou since her father insisted on announcing when the picking would be the easiest. He had good neighbors. Spread out down the waterway, they kept an eye out for each other.

Lola used her key to the camp's door and let herself in. Since it was only noon, she could wait the hour for him to get back. She put the

55

stew in the fridge and grabbed a soda at the same time. She went to through the back door and sat on the swing on the deck.

As the wind caressed her face, Lola heard the water lapping along the shoreline. She pushed off with her feet and set the swing moving. She could do with an hour of peace and quiet. Looking over the marsh, the breeze brought a balm to her spirit.

27.4N, 87.2W. 95 MPH. 252 miles southeast of Rienville.

Glancing away from the computer screen in the Wisteria Realty office, Rose picked up her cell phone and hit her husband's number on speed dial.

"Hey. Looks like Stella is heading toward Mobile." She tossed an old note into the recycling bin.

That still has us on the good side of the storm. Patrick would consider the prospect of having to leave less urgent.

"What's your feel for things?" he asked his wife. "You're the one with the business deals hanging in the air."

Taking a sip of her ever-present mug of hot tea, Rose looked back at the screen.

"Let's hold off loading up the car for a bit. If the storm keeps steering toward Alabama, we should be fine."

"You're the family meteorologist. We move on your call. Just give me a few hours' notice. I don't want to get stuck with the yahoos."

"Heard and acknowledged. We can talk more tonight." Their conversation turned to plans for the evening. After deciding on leftovers from the fridge for dinner, Rose signed off.

I don't feel totally comfortable staying, but the radar doesn't lie. Rose looked at the weather website's long-distance radar of the Gulf of Mexico. Stella was putzing away in the Gulf and simply meandering. Would she peter out to nothing except some showers or decide to gear up and move on down the road. She loved looking at the spaghetti models, as the storm track predictions were known along the coast. The cone of possibility for landfall had narrowed from Houston to the Alabama/Florida border. It's part of why storm forecasting had always fascinated her. Right now, the storm's path for the next 24 hours resembled a bundle of colorful yarn that had been attacked by a kitten.

Taking a minute, she texted Lola and Katie with the latest coordinate news and to let them know, that for the time being, the Marinos were sticking around.

*

Lola heard the put-put-put of a motor coming down the bayou and slowed the swing to a stop. As she looked over the weathered railing, she saw Spot standing in the bow of her father's green and cream bass boat, her tail wagging and tongue hanging out. Her father's constant companion looked like a proud canine version of the figurehead on the front of a Viking ship.

James was driving the boat from the steering wheel amid ship. Lola's father used the boat more for visiting his neighbors on the bayou than for fishing. She headed down the stairs at the back of the house and onto the pier. As the boat coasted into the dock, she reached down to tie up the front, Lola received a wet kiss from Spot for her assistance.

"Been visiting?" She finished the midshipmen's hitch knot on the pilling and watched Spot jump onto the dock.

"Just checking on folks. Most are staying put for the time being." James lifted a small basket and two life jackets out of the boat.

Ah, clues to his afternoon activities.

"Got any goodies left in the basket?" Lola grabbed the jackets and threw them over her shoulder.

"There's a little cheese left and part of a loaf of French bread. We pretty much finished off the rest." James finished tying up the back of the boat before heading toward the house.

Lola knew that Ms. Beryl was known for her homemade French bread. She was surprised there was even a crusty end left.

"How's Ms. Beryl?" Lola kept her head down as the wind had picked up and a few strands were blowing into her eyes. As she peered up, Lola could see her dad had a slight smile on his face as he started up the stairs. The black dog almost took her owner out at the knees in her haste to get to the door, and subsequently her food bowl, first.

"She's fine. I helped her put storm shutters on some of her windows just in case she'll need them."

Lola put the basket on the kitchen counter. She took out the container of herbed goat cheese, pulled off a handful of fresh bread and slathered on the cheese. *There are few foods on earth as good as this,* she imagined as she took a bite.

Weathering the Storm

"What's the latest on the storm? Ms. Beryl's satellite dish stopped working and her radio signal isn't strong." James sat on one of the stools in front of the kitchen counter and watched his daughter enjoy the simple snack. For a moment, Lola looked like a younger version of her mother, with her windblown hair and bright eyes.

"Rose, our personal weather guru, tells me the experts say Mobile. Her gut is telling her Stella will land closer to here." She brushed the crumbs from her hands and put the rest of the cheese in the frig. She grabbed another soda and took a drink.

"Rose has been known to be on the mark most times. Any sign of the Angel of Death?" James smiled. It was a big joke since Hurricane Katrina that you did not want to be anywhere near where a certain national network meteorologist reported from because he liked to be in the eye of every storm. The Weather Channel star was like a disaster junkie or a voodoo doll, take your pick.

"No, the Weather Channel has not said where he's heading as of a few hours ago. They don't even know which way this storm is going to go. It's just sitting out there, mocking us."

James rose from the counter and moved across the living room to the radio. He turned it to the local news channel and listened for a minute. Over the years, he had found them to have the best information about bad weather heading their way, without the sensationalism of the national media. At the moment, it was just one of the regular hosts, taking calls from people about the one thing they would grab before anything else in case they had to evacuate. James turned the sound down. They'd announce the latest coordinates at the top of the hour, along with any updates.

"So, what's your game plan Dad?" It was the elephant in the room. Lola knew it needed to be said.

"Same as always. I'll stay put unless it's a 3 or bigger. No need to leave." He sat in his recliner. Spot left Lola's side in the kitchen and moved toward her master. She put her big head on James' knee. Automatically, the man started to scratch his old friend behind the ears.

"There's no need to stay even for a 1 Dad. When the wind starts to pick up, you should come into town and stay with us. If Stella becomes a real threat here, you can head north with us too." Lola eased into the big comfy lounge chair her Dad had brought from his old house. It had been her favorite reading chair growing up and it still gave her a sense of home when she sank into it.

"No need to uproot Spot here or mess with the schedule at your house. We're high up, we've got a vented generator and plenty of food and water. We've sat through storms before and this one is no different." He showed a calmness that Lola wished she could feel.

"You know it would be a load off my mind to have you off the water during the worst of it," Lola muttered in exasperation. "I'll have enough on my plate worrying about the kids without having to think about you out here."

"I keep saying there is no need to worry. We'll deal with what comes our way," he said as he continued to rub Spot's silky ears.

"You could bring Ms. Beryl. It would be good to have her in town as well and we have the room." Now Lola had showed her hand at her level of concern for her father. Lola believed Beryl Brown to be a delightful woman. She still wasn't sure she was the right woman for her Dad.

Quiet, kind and a pleasure to be around, she was also the first woman her father had spent time with of any consequence since her mother had died. At first, Lola had been uncomfortable around the woman. It took her daughter Roslyn to tell her she was being silly and a bit unfair to Grandpa that Lola had to agree it would be ok for her father to have a lady friend. It would not mean, Roslyn stated strongly as she hugged her mother's waist, that he had loved Grandma any less.

"Let's not go to extremes just yet," her grinning father told his cautious daughter. James knew his lovely neighbor was still a touchy subject for Lola. "If Ms. Beryl doesn't want to ride out the storm alone, she can come stay with Spot and me. Give us both some credit that if it really looks bad, we'll head inland."

Weathering the Storm

Taking another swig of her soft drink, Lola was ready to call a retreat. He was old and experienced enough to ride out a storm if his building stayed upright and didn't take water. And if the surge overtook the former camp at its height, everyone in Rienville had better be north of the interstate because it would look like a tsunami had hit the town.

"Keep listening to Rose and keep me posted. I trust her internal radar more than anything. Now we just wait and see." The old man continued to look out over the water. Lola dropped the conversation and joined him gazing at the bayou.

*

On her way home from her father's house, Lola stopped at the boardwalk. It was one of her favorite places. Owned by the Nature Conservancy, it was a simple wooden walkway that reached into a section of the Honey Island Swamp.

When the kids were little, Lola would bring them here for an easy field trip. As they would walk through the lush marsh grass and bald cypress trees and head over the water, there was always something interesting for the children to see. Moving from one side to the other of the wooden walkway and peering through the fence slats, Roz and Rey would point out the turtles on the sunken logs and snowy egrets walking along the bank. In the wintertime, they would look for the bald eagles that nested in the tallest trees. If the kids saw one of the resident alligators, the day was deemed a success. On many trips, it would take some time to finally make it to the boardwalk's end.

Lola was still amazed at the changes Katrina had made to the area. Where it used to be more overgrown with majestic cypress trees and wild swamp flowers, it was now, for the most part, a vast open lake. *Still beautiful*. Lola lingered and watched a great blue heron take off from one of the small islands off to her right and glide across the water. *Beautiful, but very, very different. What will Stella do to it.*

With a shake of her head, Lola turned to walk to her car. There was no hurry really. The important stuff was packed if they needed to leave and the proverbial hatches had been battened down as much as they could be without turning the house into a cave.

It was now a waiting game for the Normandy household. Lola really hated this part. It was one of the reasons why she always said she'd take a tornado over a hurricane any day. With the inland twisters, the radar would show the storm front coming. They'd watch for the swirly icon to pop up on the TV screen and then pay attention to the names of the towns and neighborhoods in its path. It would either pass by or hit. A few hours later, it was over and you either dealt with the peace or the damage. None of these long days, sitting on pins and needles.

As she neared the end of the boardwalk, three cars drove up and parked next to her car. Out streamed half a dozen young adults. Lola always thought it would be a great place for a party, if not for the mosquitos after dark and as long as the game warden didn't catch them after the park closed. They opened the cars' trunks and started carrying boxes toward her. As they passed Lola, a young couple in shorts and t-shirts with brooms started sweeping the pine needles from the wooden walkway.

It was then that she noticed one of the young women. She too was dressed in shorts and a cotton top. The difference was her dark brown hair was styled with intricate braiding and a bright rhinestone clip on one side. She was talking quietly to a young man, pointing toward the workers.

Something was up and Lola's curiosity could not be contained as she walked toward her car and the young couple.

"You might tell those guys it's no use sweeping up the needles now. The storm will just put them back again," Lola shared a grin with the couple as she paused at her car. They laughed and the man squeezed the woman's hand before he went off to the others.

"We're getting married here in a few hours." The bride-to-be beamed, as her eyes followed her groom toward the boardwalk.

Weathering the Storm

"Best wishes to you both. You picked a beautiful spot." Lola remembered not to say 'congratulations' to a bride. She had not known the area was available for weddings, although she had seen couples posing for photos here on occasion.

"We're supposed to get married next weekend, but this storm has us worried." The young woman moved to the front of her car. "Our church isn't available today and it flooded back in Katrina. Since we planned on a small family ceremony and everyone lives here, we thought, why not?" She grabbed a box of silk flowers.

"I think that's a great idea, but I don't envy you having to change all your plans."

"My Mom has been great. She and her sisters know everyone and started calling people last night. Since the reception was going to be a pot luck dinner at my parent's house anyway, it's all good." The sounds of laughter floated to them from the boardwalk, as the decorators fought the breeze to tie white tulle to the fence posts.

"Well, I know you will have a beautiful ceremony. This is one of the prettiest places in the parish. You might even have a few herons in the background in your photos." Lola grinned as she opened her car door.

"Wouldn't that be great!" Her smile rivaled the sunshine as she walked toward her groom.

28.0N, 87.9W. 97MPH. 192 miles southeast of Rienville. The National Hurricane Center has upgraded Hurricane Stella to a Category 2 storm, with sustained winds of 97 miles per hour. Interests on the Gulf Coast should prepare for the storm to make landfall somewhere between Mobile, Alabama and Avery Island, Louisiana.

In the darkness, the contrary woman soaked up the heat from the warm Gulf waters as if she was lounging in a hot bubble bath. It rejuvenated her and gave her a second wind. Feeling the cool front from the north begin to dissipate and the late summer heat return, she made the turn toward the northwest and headed toward the Big Easy. It was time to get the party started.

28.1N, 88.0W. 97 MPH. 184 miles southeast of Rienville.

Rose awoke to the sound of the limbs from the crepe myrtle scratching against the window. The moon was shining through the banks of clouds as they passed ever so slowly over the house heading north. The wind had picked up some since they went to bed.

She worked her legs out from around the dogs lying on the comforter and got out of bed. Patrick was oblivious in his dreams. Without disturbing the quiet, Rose made her way from the bedroom to the back door. Slipping out onto the patio, she settled into one of the white rocking chairs she loved. They had left them out while putting the other patio furniture into the storage shed. If Stella arrived here, these chairs could be moved into the kitchen and used for stress relief.

The wind was blowing hard enough to make the myrtles drop some of their pretty pink blossoms unto the grass. The air was warm, and Rose could feel the difference in the humidity from earlier in the evening. Most importantly, she could smell a hint of salt in the air. Between that and the clouds, Rose knew something had changed out over the Gulf. *Seems that Stella might have changed her mind about visiting Alabama.*

Quietly, she rocked on the tiled patio and listened to the narrow-mouthed toads singing from the soggy section in the back of the yard. The light wind kept the mosquitos away. As the chair moved back and forth, she gathered up the peace that came with the rhythm. Rose would store the memories of peaceful times for the coming hectic days. In a way, she was glad the storm seemed to have chosen its path. The waiting to know it was coming this way was sometimes worse than the actual arrival.

In the morning, she'd check the professionals' opinions on how strong Stella would be and then make the decision to stay or go.

Gertie Mae came out the doggie door to check on the woman who fed her and to go do her business. When the scruffy dog made her way onto the patio, she paused in front of Rose as if to say, 'you comin'?' Rose loved this dog and her no-nonsense attitude. Rose found it easy to imagine Gertie Mae as a reincarnation of a very practical woman.

Smiling at the dog, Rose got up from the rocker and they walked into the kitchen together. Heading back to bed, she listened to the small snores coming from the dogs and her husband.

It must be nice to sleep without a care in the world. But then, Rose couldn't change the path of the storm. She could just be prepared to meet her. She laid down and snuggled into the dog pile that was her bed and fell easily back to sleep.

28.4N, 88.4W. 95 MPH. 153 miles southeast of Rienville.

Katie had finished dressing for work and was putting her hair up in a ponytail when the alarm on her nightstand went off. When she got out of bed this morning, she had reset the alarm for 7:30 a.m. to make the call to Rose's oncologist's office.

She went to the kitchen counter and read the number off the note Rose had given her before they parked at the sand bag station. Katie heard two rings before a friendly voice answered.

"Dr. MacDermitt's office."

"This is Katie Woodruff. I was told to call this morning to arrange an appointment with Dr. MacDermitt."

"Yes, Ms. Woodruff. This is Margie. I've got a note here that you would be calling. Would you be available to come in at the end of office hours today?"

"Of course. Our office is shutting down for the rest of the week and we'll be working late. I'll make sure I can leave. What time?" Katie could hear papers being shuffled in the background.

"We'll be here late as well. Can you make it at 6:30 p.m.? Our office is in Room 503 in the Physician's building."

"I'll be there." Katie proceeded to answer Margie's questions so the elusive medical results could be obtained before the meeting.

"Thank you so much for fitting me in." Katie felt her stress level lighten with the appointment made.

"No problem. See you this evening." The office manager was off to her next patient before Katie could disconnect the call.

Katie took a deep breath, grabbed her car keys and purse and left the house. She had hours to pass before, Katie hoped, she could get answers about her stay in her personal purgatory.

*

Lola picked up the phone but did not press the answer button. She was almost finished reading the local section of the paper over her morning soft drink. The talk show hosts droned on softly from the radio sitting on the kitchen counter about having a game plan.

She waited until it was past the fourth ring, usually the sign that it was not a robo-call. "Good morning," she answered.

"I'm thinking Stella is the real deal," Rose said, as Lola looked out the window at the tree branches moving with more animation than the day before.

"The radio is still saying Mobile as of this morning." Lola had had her radio on since dawn. She'd awaken early and couldn't settle enough to go back to sleep.

"I know, but I am giving you the official Rose's Foul Weather Warning. I think she's going to be coming this way and we need to seriously consider bugging out." Even with her quirky phrases, Lola sensed Rose was not messing around.

"Okay then. I'll talk to Rene and see when we can head north. Just about everything is ready and waiting in a pile by the front door."

"Good. I promised Katie a call if we decided to leave. I don't know when her office is closing."

"Sounds good. Keep us posted." Lola hung up and walked down the hallway toward Rene's home office. He wasn't traveling because the storm was wreaking havoc on the airline schedules and he didn't want to get stuck away from home. They'd decide on when to leave and then she'd call her Dad.

*

Katie received a text from Rose asking Katie to please call when she had a moment. *It will be a while*. She waded through the patient files on her desk. Her boss had decided over the weekend to close the office for the rest of the week since the possibility of the storm coming this way was high. Too late to cancel the Monday morning patients, everyone was scrambling in an orderly fashion to handle the regular workload, as well as call those patients scheduled for the rest of the week.

Katie quickly responded 'OK' to the text before she slipped her old flip phone into her scrubs pocket.

Weathering the Storm

"I know it's crazy now, but I am soooo excited about our little mini-vacation," whispered June, one of the other office staff. The young woman had just started in the office a few weeks ago and thought everything was an adventure.

That might be a good way of looking at things. Katie completed another insurance claim online.

When all the employees had arrived this morning, the staff meeting went from rather gloomy to just short of a party. Dr. Tucker had announced her decision to be proactive and shut down the office for the rest of the week. The dentist was also a mother with a young daughter and said she planned to leave the area. Laughingly, the doctor said the thought of no electricity or running water with a 9-month-old in diapers did not sound fun to her and she planned on being on the road in the morning.

What had the staff practically dancing in the aisles was Dr. Tucker had also announced everyone would be paid for their scheduled hours for the rest of the week. The practice's previous owner had not felt the same and the office workers had had to scramble to make up for the lost wages during previous storm closings.

"I'm not going to wait for the parish to decide if we should stay or go," she had said. "I think it will be easier on all of us if we handle today as usual and make the calls to cancel the appointments set for the rest of the week. Offer to reschedule the appointments when you call and we'll sort the rest of it all out when we get back," Dr. Tucker said from the front of the office's break room. "I know the extra calls are a lot of work and I appreciate your efforts. The important thing is for all of you to be safe so we can all be here next week." Her staff had showed their appreciation with thank yous before quickly getting back to work.

"It is nice to not have to worry about work. Will you stay?" Katie pulled another patient folder off a stack. Dressed in matching scrubs, June was inputting information into the patient portal, sending out a message about the office closing.

"Sort of. We live near the lake front, so we drive up to Bush to stay with my grandparents until the storm passes. They don't usually have flooding issues. They just have to deal with winds knocking down the pine trees. They have a generator so we will have power. Storms for us are like impromptu family reunions." June smiled. "What about you? Do you have family around here?"

"No. I plan to head to Nashville to see my parents for a few days."

No big family reunion. Just a quiet, probably rather tense, visit. As busy as they had been, this was the first Katie had thought about her test results all day.

"Well, what they say is true. If you are going to leave, leave early. Once they start emptying New Orleans, the roads clog fast and then it's no fun. Make sure your gas tank is full and you have a book on the passenger seat. It helps to pass the time if the traffic slows to a crawl." June gave her a quick grin and turned back to start typing at her computer. If Katie had it right, June was humming a Jimmy Buffet song about a hurricane party.

"I need a quick break. Need anything from the vending machines?" Katie rose from her office chair and headed toward the door.

"No, I'm good." June did not look up from the screen.

"Okay. I'll be back in a few minutes," Katie went through the door toward the soda machines. She called Rose to tell her the good news.

"Hurricane Central," Rose answered when Katie's call went through.

"That's a funny way to answer your phone." Katie made her selection from the machine's offerings. She predicted it would be the first of many today, caffeine being a key ingredient to get everything done that needed to happen before the office closed for the week.

"Sorry. Wasn't paying attention to the ring tone. It's a little joke between me and Patrick. He likes to think of me as his personal weathergirl."

"No problem. So, what's the word?" Katie hadn't had a storm update since her drive in to work this morning.

Weathering the Storm

"I recommend you make plans to head out. I think the official word is going to be changing soon. My gut tells me Stella is heading this way. She may not be a big storm, but she's going to be a trouble maker."

"Well, I have good news on that front. Dr. Tucker is closing the office for the rest of the week. We are trying to reach all the patients she has scheduled for the next few days. It's a mad rush to get everyone contacted. When we're done, I'll be free to leave, and I think I'll be heading out in the morning or maybe later in the day. I'd like to be in Nashville before dark." Katie took a deep breath before continuing. "And, ta-da! She's going to pay us for the time off this week! Can you believe it?"

"Smart woman, your Dr. Tucker. Good employees are hard to find, and loyalty is an even more valuable commodity. That's wonderful for you."

"It is a relief to not have to worry about dipping into my savings." Katie uncapped her soda and took a sip.

"On a different note, did you call Dr. MacDermitt's office?" Rose asked gently.

"I did. My appointment is at 6:30 p.m. tonight." Katie lowered her voice while looking down the hall to see if anyone was close by.

"That's good. I hope he has good news for you."

"At this point, I would be happy with just some information. I really appreciate the help Rose. "

"No problem. Talk to you soon." Rose hung up the phone as Katie started back for her office, mentally checking the packing list for her trip.

*

Lola checked with Rene to see if he had heard from the kids. Of course not, he said, why would they call?

"You'd think they'd be worried about their poor, ol' parents with a storm in the Gulf," she groaned as she leaned against the door frame going into his office.

Blue was sleeping soundly on his dog bed in the corner. Lola felt sad looking at the single dog in the bed he used to share with his buddy Roscoe. Although their ancient mutt had been gone two months, it was still weird to see the one small dog in the jumbo size bed.

"They are busy with their own lives. Unless the school closes for the storm, they probably don't even know Stella's in the Gulf." Rene continued to input information into the computer program. "Since Stella is leaning more toward Mobile, they probably won't close the campus in Baton Rouge."

"I'm going to call them." Lola pulled her cell-phone out of her pocket, pulling up her favorites list.

"Good luck with that." Rene chuckled as his hands continued to fly over the keyboard. "Like they're going to answer you. Ha!" He glanced up at Lola. "How long have they been your children?"

Lola tapped her finger on Rey's contact and listened to it ring. Reynard was their oldest and a senior at Louisiana State. He hoped to take his double major in biology and business and start his own microbrewery. The call went to voice mail, no surprise there for Lola and she left a message. Next, she looked up Roslyn's number and went through the same drill. Their daughter was also a student at the Baton Rouge campus working toward a physical therapist degree. Three years her brother's junior, Rey and Roz rarely crossed paths at the school. Lola liked that they were both in one place and close enough to help each other in a pinch.

After leaving basically the same voicemail for their daughter, Lola ended the call. She heard Rene try hard to muffle his mirth.

"What?" Lola attempted not to smile.

"Nothing." Rene did not look up. In the corner, Blue continued to dream doggie dreams.

"They should answer their phones." Lola frowned as she looked down at the time on her phone. *Neither of them should be in class right now.* She tried to remember their schedules.

Weathering the Storm

"They have lives of their own." Rene looked up and saw his wife's face show more concern than was warranted. Putting up a hand, Rene offered his wife an olive branch. "But I do agree with you that they should answer the phone when we call. Try sending them a text. I have found they answer those faster."

"Huh" Lola huffed, as she opened message screens for her children and used the voice button to dictate the messages.

"No emergency. Call your Mother." Lola said into the phone. She looked at the screen to make sure the auto-correct didn't think she said something totally off the wall. Lola hit the send button. If their children wanted venison stew the next time they came home for the weekend, they'd better answer in a timely manner. Lola silently left Rene's office and moved down the hall to her quilting room.

28.4N, 88.5W. 100 MPH. 148 miles southeast of Rienville.

In the early afternoon, the parish president called a press conference broadcast on all the local news channels. Rose listened to the talk radio program as she put the last check marks on her client to do list. Everything in the local real estate market was essentially on hold for the duration. Rose heard him declare a voluntary evacuation of the parish effective immediately. The information he, and other parish presidents, had received stated that Stella was going to make herself known somewhere along the Louisiana Gulf Coast in the next 72 hours as either a Category 1 or 2 storm, possibly a 3. He urged people living in low lying areas to move to higher ground and prepare for damage from a strong storm surge.

Rose knew what was coming next. Orleans Parish was also issuing an evacuation order. That meant in the next 24 hours the interstates running through Rienville were going to get very busy. They needed to leave soon. As she reached for her cell phone to give the nod to Patrick to leave, the home phone rang.

"Marino residence." Rose hoped she would not hear the telltale click signaling a tele-marketer was on the line.

"Rose? Hi, this is Judy from church. How you doing Darlin'?" Judy and Rose were part of the senior citizen outreach team at church. The group checked on the elderly in the congregation with phone calls and visits.

"I'm good Judy, considering this crazy storm. What can I do you for?"

"Have you by chance talked with Helena lately?" Rose thought the woman sounded concerned. Judy helped out the group by making phone calls to the seniors. It was a way she could serve as she was basically homebound herself taking care of her elderly husband with dementia.

"I have not. Why?"

"I've been trying to get her on the phone for two days with no luck. The last time we spoke, she mentioned she was concerned about the hurricane coming and not being able to leave. I know her family is way up in Jackson and she didn't think they would come and get her."

Lovely. Rose wondered what could possibly be more important than picking up your eighty-five-year-old mother for a hurricane and

Weathering the Storm

having her visit for a week or so? Rose tried to understand they might have their reasons, but it was hard.

"I know you're really busy Rose, but do you think you could run by Helena's house and check to see if she's there? If she doesn't answer the door, there's a back-door key under the gnome on the back patio. I'd feel better knowing they changed their mind and came and got her."

Rose calculated the trip to Helena's house. It would take fifteen minutes to get to the woman's little house near Rose's office in the older section of Rienville.

I can give the house a quick check, call Judy back with an all clear and be home within the hour.

"Sure. I'll run by and then give you a call. Are you going to be able to leave soon?"

"We'll be staying here," Rose heard Judy say softly. "Bob doesn't do well in places he doesn't know. Before the winds really whip up, our grandson Thomas will come over and stay with us to help."

"Okay, that's good to know. I'll head over there now and call you. Talk to you soon." Rose replaced the handset onto its cradle. Ruby looked up from her green doggie couch as Rose got up from her chair. Ruby was her shadow when Rose was in the house. She, along with her dog siblings had comfy beds throughout the house, as well as in Patrick's gunsmithing shop.

She tossed her slippers in the closet and tied on her tennis shoes. Rose and Ruby left through the back door to make their way to the workshop out back. Rose would let Patrick know she'd be gone about an hour and give him the all clear to start packing the car.

*

Katie was walking to the vending machine for another caffeine fix while she looked up her parent's number on her cellphone's speed dial.

She almost missed her Mom's hello when the twenty-ounce bottle rumbled down the machine's dispensing slot.

"Hey Mom." Katie pocketed the change and moved off into a corner of the break room.

"How are you doing? Is it bad down there yet? We've been watching the news." Katie imagined her Mom, Deborah Woodruff, was probably sitting in her kitchen in Nashville.

"Actually, it's rather pleasant at the moment. It's very breezy so it keeps the heat and the bugs down. But I understand it won't be fun in a few days. Looks like I'll be heading your way in the morning." Katie took a sip as she paced around the small room to look out the window toward the parking lot.

"We'll be here, and your room is always ready. I'm glad you're coming home. I don't like the idea of you being down there by yourself then the storm hits."

"Well, I just wanted to give you a head's up. I've got to get back to my desk. The office is going to be closed starting tomorrow so we have to finish cancelling appointments. I'll be working late, but I plan to get up early and will head your way. I'll call you when I'm on the road."

"Sound's good. Just be careful and take your time."

"OK. Talk to you soon. I love you guys," Katie said quietly, as a few of her co-workers walked in the door.

"Love you too Hun. We'll see you tomorrow," Deborah said before she hung up the receiver.

Katie disengaged the call as she waved to the other women in the room and went out the door. She thought about the phone call to the doctor's office earlier that morning. She had told Rose any news was welcome. She prayed it was good news. If not, at least she could share bad news with her parents in person when she got to Nashville the next day.

Katie took another drink from her umpteenth soda for the day.

Showtime. Katie walked back to her desk.

*

Weathering the Storm

Rose, once again in Patrick's clunker of a truck, drove into Helena's driveway and turned off the ignition. This morning's issue of the local paper was still in the front yard. As she got out of the truck, she picked up the plastic covered paper. Rose became uneasy at the sight of the unclaimed newspaper. From experience, she knew Helena was sort of a newspaper junkie and did nothing before reading her beloved paper with her morning coffee. It was how Helena started every day.

Maybe she's already on her way north.

During that thought, Rose noticed the mailbox door was slightly open. Walking over to the cute box with colorful flowers painted on its white surface, Rose opened the door to find letters and an oversized mailing bag stuffed inside.

It was too early for today's mail, so this had to be from yesterday. I hope she arranged for someone to pick up her mail while she's gone. Since nothing else would fit in the mailbox, Rose emptied the box. She closed the mailbox door tightly and headed for the front door.

Ringing the doorbell didn't bring a response, so Rose loudly rapped a few times on the screen door. Still no answer. The curtains where pulled across the front windows, blocking any view of the inside. Wanting to be able to tell Judy all was well, Rose walked around the house and through the gate in the chain link fence onto the back patio. She knocked on the back door and tried peeking through the ruffled curtain on its window.

No answer.

In for a penny, in for a pound. Juggling the armload of mail, Rose turned around to find the key concealing gnome. Surrounded by a pool of vibrant flowering impatiens, the statue resembled a little rascal playing a game of hide and seeks in the garden. Rose lifted the little guy and retrieved the small key enclosed in a small Ziploc bag. Moving back to the house, she slipped the key into the lock, turned the handle and opened the door.

Sticking her head in the doorway, she yelled, "Hello Helena? It's Rose Marino." No response from the interior of the house.

"Helena." Rose called again as she entered the small kitchen. The house was still. Rose felt a bit creepy walking into the place, although she had visited the older woman on several occasions. Helena had shared many stories from Rienville's history with Rose over a cup of hot tea with honey.

Rose spotted a worn, leather purse on the kitchen counter. Rose recognized it from seeing Helena at church and around town.

Nope, no woman leaves town without her purse.

Moving into the living room, Rose let loose a startled yelp as she found Helena lying between the couch and the coffee table. Quickly walking around the table, she kneeled down by Helena's head and spoke to the woman softly.

"Helena, it's Rose. Can you hear me?" She pushed the hair back from the woman's face gently while she tried not to move her. There was no response although her cheek was warm under Rose's hand.

Looking up, she saw an old-fashioned almond colored desk phone on an end table by a recliner. She stood and moved quickly. The handset was heavy as she dialed 911.

"911, what is your emergency?"

"My friend is unconscious. Her name is Helena Guici and I am at her house. We need an ambulance. She is 85 years old. I don't know the address here." All the information rushed out of Rose's mouth on one breath.

"Okay. I have this call coming from 625 South St. and I have an ambulance in route." The operator said in a calm voice. "What is your name?"

"Yes, she lives on South St. She's not moving," Rose looked worriedly over at her friend.

"Can you see if she is breathing? Is she bleeding?"

"Yes, she's breathing, and I don't see any blood."

"Okay. Ma'am, what's your name?" the dispatcher asked again.

"Rose Marino." Rose took another deep breath and watched Helena's chest for movement. It was there, but faint.

Weathering the Storm

"Ms. Marino, are there any pets in the house that need to be put up before the paramedics arrive?"

"No, no pets. You said they are on their way. When will they get here?" Now that she had someone to help her, even by phone, Rose became less frantic. She even felt a little irritated by the woman's calm attitude on the other end of the phone.

Doesn't she understand we need to do something here? Now? It was then that Rose heard a faint siren coming from down the street.

"Ms. Marino, the paramedics should be arriving now. Can you please open the front door and direct them to your friend? Don't hang up. I'll stay on the line until they are in the house."

"Okay. I'll be back." Since the old phone was still connected to the base by a cord, Rose laid the phone down on the table and paused at Helena's form on the floor.

She quickly knelt down to her old friend before going to the door.

"The paramedics are here sweetheart. I'm letting them in now." Rose spoke quietly. She didn't know if the woman could hear her, but it made Rose feel better just thinking she could.

She moved to the front door and opened it to find the ambulance parked on the street and a man and a woman in green uniforms walking up the front path carrying cases that reminded Rose of Patrick's tackle boxes.

"Thank you for coming so fast. She's in the den." Rose held the door open and pointed to the right as they walked past her into the foyer. Moving into the den, they put down their cases and moved the coffee table away from their patient.

"What's her name?" The woman paramedic looked at Helena's face and felt for a pulse in her neck. Her nametag read 'Merrick'.

"Her name is Helena Guici. I believe she's 85 years old. A friend asked me to stop by and check on her since she hadn't heard from her in two days. We thought her family had decided to come and get her because of the storm." When Rose finished talking, the woman started

79

speaking to Helena in a loud voice while the other medic was feeling her arms and legs for breaks.

"Do you know how long she's been unconscious? Does she have any health problems?" The male paramedic asked as he gently rolled the patient over onto her back. His partner placed a blood pressure cuff on Helena's arm and started pumping the rubber bulb in her hand as she put the stethoscope ends into her ears.

"I don't know. We have a buddy system at church to check on our older members. Her buddy could not reach her yesterday or this morning so she called to see if I could check on her. She's never mentioned any serious illnesses." Hearing a murmuring noise coming from the side of the room, Rose noticed the phone receiver still sitting on the end table. She picked it up.

"I'm sorry. I forgot to get back to you. The paramedics are here."

"That's no problem. You can hang up now. Good luck." The dispatcher disconnected the call. Rose replaced the handset on its cradle.

The paramedics had hooked Helena up to a machine and she could see different numbers and lines showing up on a boxed monitor. Based on her limited knowledge from medical dramas on television, Rose didn't know if the squiggles held good news of bad.

"What is your name?" the man asked. His nametag read 'Smith'.

"Rose Marino." She stood off to the side of the fireplace and out of the way.

"Okay Ms. Marino, can you please go to the refrigerator and look for her Vial of Life bottle." Smith said as he continued to work.

"Her what?" Rose moved toward the kitchen.

"It's called a Vial of Life. Looks like an extra-large prescription bottle for horse pills. It's a program the fire department has for senior citizens and other people with health issues. It should have her medical information listed inside. There's a sticker on her front door saying she's in the program. Please check her frig."

Sorting through jars of salad dressing and pickles, she found what she was looking for. As Rose was taking the oversized yellow medicine bottle out of the refrigerator, she heard the screen door open. Looking

Weathering the Storm

around the corner, she saw a police officer shutting the door behind him.

"I'm Officer MacKenzie. I'm here about the emergency call." The man was taking a small notebook out of his shirt pocket as he approached the kitchen.

"I'm Rose Marino. I need to give this to the medics. Rose moved past the officer and into the den. She handed the bottle to Smith. As he took the plastic bottle, he saw the officer behind Rose.

"Hey Mac. Long time, no see," Smith said. "Cori can give you the particulars while I call in the stats." He turned to a cellphone as the other paramedic continued to work on her patient while she relayed the information.

"We've got a woman named Helena Guici, approximately 85 years of age. Found unconscious approximately 30 minutes ago by Ms. Marino here. There's no sign of trauma. We'll be ready to transport in a few minutes. Can you please make a check for prescription bottles around the house? She has a Vial of Life, but it hasn't been updated in two months. Don't want to miss anything new. Try the bathroom or the kitchen counter. "

"Ms. Marino, why don't you help me look and we can talk at the same time." The officer motioned Rose out of the den and into the kitchen.

"Tell me how you came to be here and found your friend." Officer McKenzie followed Rose down the hallway toward the master bedroom. Rose explained about the church phone program, the unclaimed newspaper and mail and the key under the gnome. Officer MacKenzie wrote down the information in his palm-size notebook.

"So, the back and front doors were locked when you got here?" Rose nodded as she saw a weekly pill box sitting on the vanity in the bathroom. She picked it up and opened the filled slots. There were three pills that looked like prescription grade medicines and what she recognized as a low dose aspirin in each slot. The pills in last night's slot were still in the box, as well as this morning's doses. She opened the medicine cabinet and saw four bottles from the local pharmacy. Removing them from the cabinet, she showed them to the officer.

"Let's take all of it into the other room and show them." As the two moved through the kitchen, the policeman motioned to the purse sitting on top of the kitchen counter. "Is that Ms. Guici's purse?"

"I believe it is."

"Please check it for any other prescription bottles. Do you have contact information for her family? Is there someone in Rienville we can call?" Rose made a quick search of the purse and didn't find any additional medications except a travel size bottle of pain relief medicine.

"There's no one living close by. I think the nearest one is her daughter living in Mississippi. I know their names, but not their phone numbers. They are probably in her phone book."

MacKenzie and Rose moved back to the den. There was now a gurney waiting in the hall. As they had passed through the kitchen, Rose had gone into the pantry and gotten a Ziploc bag for the pill box and prescription bottles.

"These were on the counter. Two of the bottles are empty so I don't know what's in the pill box. The pills for last night and this morning are still here." Rose handed the bag to Smith.

"Thanks," he said as he glanced at the box and the pill bottles. "This should help. Do you have contact info for her family?"

"She does not. We're going to look around until we can find it." The officer followed Rose as she went back into the kitchen.

Rose opened Helena's purse and got out her wallet. Inside with a few dollar bills and photos of her grandchildren, was an insurance card. She pulled it out of the windowed pocket and placed in on the table. After rooting around a minute, she found a mini address book with a rubber band holding it closed. When she opened it, Rose saw dozens of names and phone numbers, many of them crossed out and written over in the margins. It seemed obvious that Helena had used the small book for many years. Rose recognized Helena's daughter's name and

Weathering the Storm

showed it to the officer. He wrote it and the phone number on his pad along with his other notes.

"We need to contact the daughter. Would you feel comfortable making the call?" Officer MacKenzie asked as they heard the paramedics packing up their equipment to take Helena to the hospital. She was still unconscious.

Rose hesitated a moment before saying, "I can do that. What's the number?" Rose took her cellphone out of her pocket and noticed her hands were not steady. Taking a seat at the vintage formica table, she dialed the Mississippi phone number and waited for someone to answer.

"Hello?" The voice on the other end sounded hesitant. *They don't recognize my number.* "Is this June Parsons?"

Cautiously, the woman responded. "Yes. Who is this?"

"June, this is Rose Marino. I'm a friend of your mother."

"Hi Rose. My Mom has mentioned you." Rose sensed a bit of relief pass over the phone line. "What can I do for you?"

"June, I'm at your Mom's house. When I got here, I found her unconscious and called 911. The paramedics are here now."

"What? What's wrong? Is she awake now?" Rose could hear panic rising in the woman's voice. *I couldn't blame her.*

"No, she's still unconscious. Helena didn't answer her phone yesterday or today when Judy from church called. Judy asked if I could come be and check on her. We thought she might have already left for the storm. When I got here, I found her on the floor in her den and called 911. They're getting ready to take her to the hospital."

"Oh my God! Hold on a minute please," June said quietly. As Rose sat at the kitchen table, she heard June talking to someone else on her end. After a moment, Helena's daughter came back on the line.

"We're getting some things together and we'll be down there as soon as we can." Rose could tell the woman was moving around while she talked on the phone.

"They are taking her to Rienville General. Hold on a second. There is a policeman here who needs to talk with you." Rose handed the phone to the officer.

"Ms. Parsons, this is Officer MacKenzie. I heard Ms. Marino say you're heading down this way. Where are you now?"

"We live just south of Jackson, in Byram, Mississippi. Why?"

"We've gotten word they have started to activate the contraflow process on I-55. You can use the interstate to a point, and then you're going to have to use secondary roads to get into Rienville. Even with that, it's going to take you longer than usual to get here."

"Thank you. I didn't even think about that. We'll just head south however we can."

"All right. I'll let you talk to Ms. Marino. Good luck." Officer McKenzie handed the phone back to Rose.

"June. I have Helena's insurance card with me."

"Thank you. Rose, is there any way you can please stay with her until we get there? I hate for her to be in the hospital by herself. We'll get to her as fast as we can."

"Of course, I will. This is my cell phone so save this number. I need to go. They are putting your mother into the ambulance now and I want to follow them there. I'll call when there is more information."

"Thank you so very much Rose. We'll see you soon." Helena's daughter hung up the phone and Rose put her cellphone back in her pocket.

"Why don't you put the purse in Ms. Guici's bedroom so it's not sitting out on the counter and I'll help you lock up." The officer watched the gurney and a still unconscious Helena be wheeled out the front door.

"Thanks. That's a good idea." Rose moved the purse and then turned off the lights throughout the house, leaving one light on over the kitchen sink. After the officer walked through the house checking doors and windows, Rose gave him her contact information.

"The front door is locked. We'll go out the back," MacKenzie gestured toward the door.

Weathering the Storm

Rose and the officer left the way she came in and she locked the door. As they walked around to the front of the house, the officer said something into the microphone attached to his shoulder and received a coded message back.

"I hope everything works out okay for your friend," he said kindly to Rose. "Someone from the department will follow up with the hospital to make sure this was nothing more than a medical emergency."

"I really appreciate the help. Thank you." She shook the officer's hand and then moved to her truck.

Sitting down and closing the door, Rose started the engine and looked at the clock on the dash. *How could so much happen in less than an hour?* Sitting still, she said a silent prayer for Helena and her family.

When she was done, Rose pulled out her phone to give Patrick a call. They wouldn't be leaving this afternoon after all.

*

Lola finished putting the tote into the back of the SUV and sat down on the fender to take a breather. In the storage box were quilts that her mother, grandmother and Rosyln had made as well as a small one of her own. There were few things Lola would grab if the house was on fire and these were some of them. *Yes, I'm a sentimental sap and I'm OK with that.*

Swiping her sleeve over her forehead to wipe away the sweat, she rose from the back of the car and peered inside. *Quilts, check. Documents box, check. Box with photo albums, check. All we need is the overnight suitcases, Rene's briefcase, my backpack and Blue.*

If they could leave in the next hour, they could be in Tuscaloosa by dark and enjoy a late dinner in Tuscaloosa at Dreamland. Lola mentally reviewed the route they would take to Atlanta.

She got out her phone and hit James' number on speed dial. When it went to voice mail, Lola left a message for her father to call her. He was good about listening to the radio, but he may not have heard the evacuation notice.

Moving to her message's icon, she tried texting next.

'Hey Dad. Did you hear the evacuation notice?' she quickly typed and pressed send. Lola closed the back of the car and headed into the house. She had remembered she wanted to take the boxes of Girl Scout cookies in the freezer. Few things made evacuations tolerable. A box or two of caramel goodness would raise the morale in the Normandy car.

*

Katie sat in the small doctor's office, watching the crepe myrtles waltzing in the breeze just outside the window. The wind was picking up even though Stella was still a considerable distance off the coast.

She turned back toward the interior of the office. Katie noticed the walls were not covered with the obligatory diplomas and certificates hung to instill confidence in nervous patients. Instead, there were brightly framed Mardi Gras posters and photos of small groups of people dressed in a wide variety of costumes.

Her curiosity piqued, Katie got up out of the chair and moved to the wall to take a closer look. Each picture featured several adults and at least four kids. Passing from one photo to the next, the groups varied in number, while each containing the same six individuals with striking red hair. Although the shades ran from reddish gold to almost auburn, there was no mistaking they were related in some way.

As she went from photo to photo, Katie could see the years progress as the children grew taller, while the two adults changed little. In one of the pictures, everyone had the red and white striped shirts and signature hats from the Where's Waldo? books while the photo next in line on the wall featured a congregation of giant bee people. Katie smiled when she looked at another that had the flavor of medieval England and the Knights of the Round Table.

Weathering the Storm

The door opened behind her. Katie turned and watched one of the adult redheads from the photos walk into the room. The man joined Katie standing in front of the photos.

"My favorite year was when I was King Arthur," Dr. Hilliard MacDermitt said, pointing at the photo featuring a smiling man in a crown. "I got to walk around for weeks before the parade saying, 'I'm Arthur, King of the Britons'. It was a lot more fun than saying, 'Hello Ms. Woodruff, I'm Dr. MacDermitt and we need to talk about your test results." He held out his hand and Katie took it firmly.

"Fighting cancer is like slaying dragons, I would think. And please call me Katie."

"I like the analogy, Katie. Thanks."

He dropped her hand and motioned her to take a seat in one of the chairs in front of his desk. As she got comfortable in the chair, Katie was surprised to see the physician sit in the chair next to her, instead of what she viewed as the chair of intimidation behind his desk.

The physician took the stethoscope from around his neck and laid it on the desk. Then he picked up a file from the desktop, crossed an ankle over the other knee and settled the file on his lap.

"I've reviewed your records from the mammogram and the needle biopsy. The mass in your breast is five centimeters wide and a bit of a conundrum." Katie tried to lessen the gripe her hands had on the strap of her purse while the doctor continued. "It is solid and without fluid. With that being said, the needle biopsy showed no carcinoma cells. However, the quality of the cells in the fine needle biopsy was poor."

"So, what does that mean?"

"It means the test is inconclusive. I can't tell you from the biopsy that it's benign nor can I tell you it's malignant. The absence of those cells does let me lean more toward it being benign."

Katie had really been looking for more of a black and white answer.

"So, what are my options?"

"Well, you have several. You can leave it be and we can check it again in a few months. If it's benign, there shouldn't be any change and it could even be reabsorbed by your body. Or you can have a lumpectomy now and we'll slice it up five ways to Sunday and give you a definitive answer as to its status. If it turns out not to be benign, then you will have to make some choices." His monologue had been accompanied by his finger quietly tap, tap, tapping on the file on his lap.

Her eyes drifted to the photos on the wall of the doctor and his family. He followed her gaze to the pictures and started to smile.

Without looking away from the sweet shot of the giant bee people, Katie asked. "If it was your wife in the same situation, what would you advise her to do?"

The smile left his face and he looked stoic. Dr. MacDermitt turned to Katie and waited for her to look him in the eye.

"I'd yank that puppy out so fast, if would make her head spin." Then smiling he added, "Medically speaking that is."

Katie looked closely at the physician. She could see compassion as well as intelligence in his eyes.

"Yanking, medically speaking that is," Katie said with a grin, "sounds good to me. How soon can I get this done?"

"As soon as this storm passes. We should be able to set up an appointment with a surgeon for two weeks from now. The lumpectomy can be done as an out-patient surgery. You'll probably want to take a day off afterwards to rest and let the anesthesia get out of your system. If Stella passes us by, or is only bothersome, there should be no delay. Unfortunately, most offices are already closed. I can put in a message to a surgeon I work with here at the hospital and tell her we would appreciate her first available opening in the surgery schedule. We should get an answer back in a few days. How does that sound?"

"It sounds like a plan. What's the surgeon's name? I think everyone at this hospital is covered by my insurance."

Weathering the Storm

"Dr. Adrian, Dr. Gwendolyn Adrian. She's good technically. My patients tell me she's got a good way of talking to them, so her bedside manner is better than most surgeons."

"OK. Please set it up and I'll work around her schedule." Katie tried to give the doctor a look that projected more strength than what she was sure he saw from her when he walked in the door.

"All right. Let's go see Margie and she'll get the ball rolling," Dr. MacDermitt rose from the chair and directed Katie toward the door.

Time to slay some dragons, Katie thought as they went into the hall toward the receptionist's desk.

*

Lola put a briefcase in the back of the SUV. There was still quite a bit of room left in the back since the last row of seats had been laid down flat. *Blue should be comfortable.*

Thinking back, she grimaced at the memory of their packing for their trip escaping from Hurricane Katrina. Their two teenagers, a dog and at the last minute, her daughter's friend leaving with only a backpack full of clothes.

The kids had been stacked like cordwood, each with a pillow and a set of headphones. Amazingly, there had been little of the usual bickering coming from the backseat on that trip. Very unlike previous vacations. The air had been definitely different on that historic trip north.

Once again sitting on the bumper, Lola pulled out her cellphone and hit "Pop". It went straight to voicemail.

He must be talking to Ms. Beryl. Lola closed the flip top on her useful, yet antiquated phone and slipped it into her pocket. *Either that or the cell towers are already jammed to capacity.*

The wind gusts had continued to increase in the last few hours and it could now be classified as consistently windy. The tall pines swayed slowly and gracefully like dancers at a Grateful Dead concert. The news report on the hour said gusts were constant at 35 mph along the coast. Stella was still a few hundred miles offshore.

Seeing her neighbor Betty down the street, loading her car as well, Lola started walking toward her neighbor's driveway. Lola reasoned it was always good to know where everyone was going in case it was hard to get back later. She had a few minutes since Rene had run to help his friend David get his boat out of the water at the marina.

*

James pushed the 'favorites' button on his cellphone, waiting for Lola to answer the phone.

"All circuits are busy. Please try again later," came over the phone line for what seemed like the hundredth time today. He pressed the off button and closed the device.

"Did you try her home phone." Beryl walked down the hall and put the suitcase next to her front door. She had expressed surprise that James actually wanted to leave for a storm. Beryl had made a joke about needing the right motivation. James had responded 'Tru Dat' and made her smile.

"I'm so used to using this stupid phone in my pocket, I forget she has a landline." James dialed his daughter's home phone number from memory.

One ringy-dingy, two ringy-dingy. Why he was remembering that old Lily Tomlin character now, he had no idea. Lola's answering machine picked up after two rings.

"Hi. Thanks for calling. If you're selling something, hang up. If we're friends, leave a message and we'll call you back." James grinned as he waited for the beep.

"'Lola. This is your father. Beryl and I are heading out on a little trip. We'll call you when we're settled. Thought you'd be glad to know we are both off the water and Spot is with us. Take care. Love ya.' He closed the phone and slipped it into this shirt pocket.

Weathering the Storm

"OK Ms. Beryl, let's blow this popsicle stand." James picked up her suitcase while she grabbed her purse. Spot was waiting at the front door, looking forward to the ride. Unfortunately, he had lost the shotgun seat for the duration.

Beryl locked the front door and made her way to the SUV. They had moved her car to the nearest higher ground, the local grocery store parking lot, an hour ago.

All three travelers settled into their seats.

James saw Beryl take one last peak through the windshield. He hoped it made for a good memory for his friend in case it was gone after Stella's visit. He was surprised at how calm she appeared.

"It will be OK Ms. Beryl. It will be here when we get back," He shifted the gear into reverse, backed up and turned the car to head down the gravel driveway. After turning the car onto the road, James placed his hand on hers on the console and squeezed gently.

"It will be alright whether it is or isn't." She turned away from her cottage and looked down the road. "It's amazing how losing it all once makes the thought of it happening again not so horrible." She squeezed his hand back. James smiled as he looked at the strong woman sitting in his co-pilot seat.

"Move Out!" Beryl shouted. Spot responded with a bark. James just grinned as he headed for the highway.

28.5N, 89.0W. 110 MPH. 132 south of Rienville.

Finally leaving the hospital, a gust of wind flipped Katie's hair in her eyes as she made her way to the hospital parking lot. Pushing it back off her face, a flash of royal blue and red caught her attention. Recognizing the Chicago Cubs flag displayed like a prize-winning pennant on the back of Rose's husband's truck, Katie started walking in that direction. She had time since she had decided to not leave tonight.

No one was in the truck. Since it was the closest door, Katie felt drawn toward the hospital's emergency room entrance. She hoped nothing had happened to Rose or Patrick. As she entered through the automatic sliding doors, she saw Rose sitting in the corner of the sterile looking waiting room, holding a cup of coffee.

"Rose is Patrick all right?" she asked as quietly as possible while crossing the room. Rose looked up and gave her a small smile.

"He's fine. He'd better be home finishing up our packing." Rose gave her a wane smile. "I checked in on an elderly friend from church this afternoon and found her lying on the floor." Rose paused to take a sip of coffee. She proceeded to give the short version of her afternoon to Katie as they sat in the uncomfortable plastic chairs. Katie squeezed Rose's arm as she could see her friend was distressed by the day's events.

"How is she doing?" Katie looked toward the doors to the examining rooms.

"They just came out to tell me she has been going in and out of consciousness so that is improvement. They've ruled out a stroke, thank God." Rose watched as a mother and child walked in the door. The child, who looked to be about twelve years old, was cradling his right arm in his left hand, grimacing. His mother looked concerned, but calm. *Probably not her first trip here*, Rose thought.

"I told Helena's daughter I would stay until they got here. Normally, it would take about two and a half hours to drive here from their house. The police officer who came to check on the emergency call said they were starting contraflow on I-55, so they will have to take back roads for part of the way. I don't expect them for several hours yet."

"How did you know I was here?" Rose moved her attention back to her young friend.

"I was leaving the hospital and saw Patrick's truck. Thought there was a good chance one or both of you were in here. I just finished meeting with Dr. MacDermitt." Katie was grateful the waiting room was relatively empty at the moment.

Weathering the Storm

"How did it go?" Rose tentatively asked. She knew from experience this was a hard row to hoe. She set the nearly empty Styrofoam cup on the side table covered in ancient magazines.

"Not so much good news as no news. He was able to access my tests results and they were inconclusive. I have to say it is very frustrating that they can't seem to give me a straight yes or no when I ask if I have cancer." Katie blew out a big breath, making the bangs on her forehead puff up. Considering the visit happened due to Rose's efforts, she was comfortable sharing the info with her friend.

"What's your next step?" Rose asked quietly. Katie could hear the hospital intercom in the background, calling a doctor to the third floor.

"The good thing is he's leaning toward it being a benign mass rather than malignant, which made me feel better. He said I could watch it for a few months to see if it got larger or I could have it removed." The sunset outside the waiting room window was turning the color of the blood orange she had had for breakfast that morning.

"Did he offer another option?" Katie appreciated her friend's patience. She knew from their relatively short friendship that it was taking a lot of will power for Rose not to jump in and try to control things.

"I told him I did not want to sit around and do nothing. So we agreed that I would have a lumpectomy as soon as possible after the storm passes. If the post-surgical tests show it to be malignant, we'll deal with that when the time comes," Katie fought the fear that welled up in her chest. She took a deep breath and willed the tears brimming in her eyes to stay put. Even with Dr. MacDermitt's positive outlook, she realized she was still terrified inside. Rose slung an arm around her young friend, and they sat quietly for a few moments before Katie stood to take her leave.

"Well, it sounds like you're making headways and that is good. Did he recommend a surgeon?"

"Someone named Dr. Adrian," said Katie.

"I don't know the name, but I do know MacDermitt is particular about who sees his patients so he should be good."

"She actually. Dr. Gwendolyn Adrian," said Katie.

"Well, that was very politically incorrect of me, wasn't it?" Rose laughed. "Even better. I'd like to think she will be more conservative where the surgery is concerned than a man would be."

"There is that. I feel better having a plan in place. The not knowing what to do was worse before I saw him. It's not perfect, but it's OK." I really appreciate your help in getting me the appointment, Rose. It meant the world to me." Katie leaned over and gave Rose a fierce hug. Rose hugged the young woman back with equal fervor. Separating, both women smiled.

"No problem sweeting. I was glad I could help. Since they've closed your office, are you leaving tonight? Not that I like that idea." Rose had a slight frown on her face. She knew Katie was capable of getting to Nashville OK, but the thought of a single woman driver on the interstate so late at night was not a good one.

"No, I'll be up at dawn and leave then. I have no trouble waking early for a road trip. What about you?"

"Smart girl. We're going to leave at first light as well. Helena's family should be here in the next few hours and then I can head home."

"Can I get you anything? Or I could stay with you?" Katie paused in her walk toward the door.

"No, I'm good. They said they would be admitting her and moving her to a regular room within the hour. Patrick is bringing me a book to help pass the time and a snack."

Moving across the waiting room, Rose gave Katie another hug. The younger woman promised she'd call and check on her later. Rose hugged her back and wished her a bon voyage.

"Humor an old girl and give me a call when you get to Nashville, OK?" Rose asked as Katie started to leave.

"You're not old, but I can humor you anyway. Be safe on the road. Tell Patrick I said Hey."

Weathering the Storm

"You be safe too. Give Lola a call with your news if you have a moment. She'll want to know the latest as well. It really does sound like as good of news as you could have received. Hold on to that."

"I'll give her a call," Katie waved back at her friend as she moved through the exit. A gust of wind moved the public health posters on the inside wall as the automatic doors slid closed. Stella was moving closer.

*

Lola wrapped up her chat with Betty and wished her safe travels to Senatobia. Rene had returned from the marina a few minutes ago. Lola crossed the driveway and walked toward the front door. As she saw the door open, she saw a blinding flash in her peripheral vision, followed almost immediately by a tremendous explosion. Instinctively, Lola threw her hands over her head and started to crouch down against the brick wall by the door.

"What the hell?" she heard Rene yell. Rene had been opening the front door for his wife when the explosion lit the cul-du-sac. He flew out the door and put his arms around Lola, covering both their heads as best he could, and he pushed her to the pavement. Lola's bare arms scrapped against the brickwork and she could hear her heartbeat racing in her ears.

Another flash then a boom sounded. Both people cringed as they stayed as low as possible. They remained that way for what seemed to Lola like a very long time although it was probably less than a minute. Lola felt Rene pull away from her and then slowly get up, his knees creaking.

"Transformer," he said as he helped Lola stand. As she brushed off the masonry grit from her arm, she thought the strawberry bruise that had started to rise on her arm would sting like a big dog later.

Looking down the street, they could see the transformer in question on fire in Mrs. Lewis' side yard. Leaning against the electric company's pole was what was left of the towering dead pine tree the neighbors had been asking her to cut down for years. Impressive flames and bright blue sparks shot from the transformer's blackened body, igniting the trees growing around the pole. Lola heard the sound of fire sirens in the distance grow stronger. A hint of flashing lights could be seen along the house rooftops toward the entrance of the subdivision.

Betty and her husband Joe had come out into their yard to see the spectacle.

"Nothing like a little excitement," a frowning Rene said as he and Lola watched the fire truck come down the street. Firefighters in full gear turned out from the large, red truck and started to pull hose from the back. One firefighter dragged a wide hose with a coupler on the end over to the hydrant in the Carter's front yard.

More neighbors come out of their homes. They simply stood by, like spectators in some reality show. Lola had always loved watching fires, a fascination she shared with her father. It was not out of the question for James, if a fire truck with lights flashing passed them on the street, to change direction and follow the truck on its call. Slightly illegal, but fun none the less for a much younger Lola.

As they watched the excitement down the street, a police car drove up and parked in front of Mrs. Lewis' house. She was standing at the curb in front of her home. Close enough to see the action, far enough away to escape if things got worse.

Quickly, the firefighters carefully doused the lower part of the dead tree and threw water on the surrounding trees and Mrs. Lewis' roof. The transformer was still energized, and Lola remembered water and electricity don't mix well.

"I guess saying 'we told you so' would not be kind at this time," Rene mumbled. He nodded toward the obviously frazzled Mrs. Lewis.

A bucket truck from the utility company drove up the street and parked just past the firetruck. The driver got out and headed toward the fire captain standing to the side, talking into his walkie-talkie.

Weathering the Storm

"Be nice," Lola said, while secreting wanting to issue the same statement. The dead tree had been a topic of conversation on their street for years.

The blackened transformer stopped sparking a few minutes later. The fire crew moved after a signal from the power company employee. Opening the valve on the high-pressure hose, they sent a rushing arc of water toward the top of the pole while also further dosing the nearby trees.

Show's over folks. Time to get back to packing. Lola moved toward the house while she shared with Rene an update on her constant worry.

"I still can't get ahold of Dad," Lola told her husband as she opened the front door and they went in. A deafening silence greeted them. No hum from the refrigerator, no news talk radio commentator sermonizing from the kitchen counter.

"Well, isn't that special? I always wondered if that transformer served our house and now, we know." Rene took in the quiet and could already feel the temperature rising inside the house.

*

James and Beryl were tooling along I-59 at a surprisingly good clip. As they drove north with many further evacuees, his phone rang in his jacket pocket. Without looking at the screen, he flipped it open.

"Coubillion." James said as he slowed down behind a semi.

"You old Goat. Where the hell are you?" a gravelly voice called from the other end of the line.

"You're an older goat than me, Bennett. I'm heading north, leaving that witch Stella behind."

"Good for you. How far down the road are you?" Bennett Finnegan was one of James' favorite people from his Air Force days.

"We just passed Poplarville on I-59."

"We? That sounds promising if you aren't talking about that old hound of yours."

"I have Ms. Beryl in the co-pilot seat. My old hound Spot takes exception to your description. Where are you?" Beryl gave him a questioning glance before looking back down at the newspaper she had been reading to him.

"I'm getting ready to take my plane out of Diamondhead to head up to Branson. Wondered if you'd like to ride along? Bennett sounded like he was walking out in the wind. His voice level came and went with the breeze.

"Sounds like a fun trip, but I don't think your plane can fit us all and where would we meet you?" He flipped his turn signal on and took the off ramp for a rest area on the side of the interstate. In a moment he was parked. Looking over at Beryl he raised a questioning eyebrow.

"The Cherokee seats six. Right now, it's just me and Lucy. I've got her kennel and could round up another for your mutt. If you didn't have a lot of luggage, I think we'd be fine. I could pick you guys up at the Hattiesburg airport. What do ya say?"

"Hold on a minute." James pressed the phone to his chest and turned to Beryl. He relayed the idea to her. "What do you think?"

"I've never flown in such a small plane. I take it you've flown with him before?" The look on Beryl's face was of cautious excitement. Her eyes were bright as she looked at her traveling companion.

"I have and he's a very steady pilot. No showboating. Since his wife died, he and his dog Lucy have made trips across the country in that plane. He's been flying all his life. I think it sounds like a great idea if you're good with it." At that moment, James realized how happy he was to have her with him, to share this type of adventure with her.

"Well, we did say this was going to be an experience. Why not?" said Beryl grinning at her partner in crime. Spot leaned over the front seat, wagging his tail and whining. He wondered why they were stopped and not making a move to take him for his usual walk.

James uncovered the phone. "Bennett, you've got a deal. We'll meet you at the airport in Hattiesburg. How long 'til you're there?" He rooted around in the back-seat foot well and came back with Spot's leash and water bowl. He handed them to Beryl, and she left the car to get the dog from the hatchback door.

"I should be there within two hours. You can park your car in long term parking. Go into the terminal and tell them you need a ride to the small craft terminal"

"OK. We'll see you there. And Bennett, we appreciate the offer."

"No problem. I should have called sooner. I just decided it might be a good idea to get the plane out. Looking forward to meeting your traveling companion and I don't mean Spot. See you in two." The call disconnected. While he had it open, James tried calling Lola again to give her an update of their plans. The 'all circuits are busy' message came on and he closed the phone.

Looking out the windshield at Beryl with the frisky dog romping from tree to tree, James smiled at this change in plans. He liked the idea of having a little more excitement in his life and he especially liked the view through his window.

*

Katie entered her cozy house. The bags she had packed for her trip to Nashville sat next to the front door. On the ride home from the meeting with Dr. MacDermitt, she had listened to the local talk radio station and was amazed at the traffic congestion already emanating from New Orleans.

As she looked out the window, the sun sank closer to the horizon. Katie watched the horizon darken from pale gold to more of the rusty orange of a faded UT t-shirt. *Perhaps this is a good omen.* It was approaching dusk.

I just can't see myself driving all night. The nine-hour drive was long enough without having to worry about traffic snarls and trying to stay awake after working all day to close the office.

Katie pulled out her cellphone from her scrubs pocket and dialed her Mom and Dad's home phone. She tried several times to get the call through the congested airwaves. Rose had warned Katie the lack of cell service would be just one of the small inconveniences found in the path of a hurricane.

Wishing she had not cancelled her home phone line, she redialed the number a few more times and finally heard an actual ring on the line.

"Woodruff residence." Katie smiled at her Mom's cheery voice.

"Hey Mom." She did her best not to sound as tired as she felt.

"Where are you sweetie? When did you leave? Your father has wanted me to call for updates and I told him not to bother you while you were driving."

"I haven't left yet. I'm still in Rienville." Katie walked around the kitchen and grabbed a glass from the cabinet for some ice water.

Katie could detect anxiety seeping into her mother's voice. Deborah Woodruff needed some clarification from her daughter.

"Katie, we've been watching the national news and they've been saying an evacuation has been ordered for your area. What are you still doing down there?"

"I got delayed at work," using part of the truth to sooth her conscience. "We needed to contact all the patients we had scheduled for the next few days to let them know we would be closed. Some of them needed medicine refills and stuff like that. Plus, the evacuation order for the New Orleans area is voluntary for now." She popped some ice cubes out of the freezer tray. *I should make a few extra trays tonight to put in her cooler in the morning.*

"I don't understand why the doctor didn't let you guys leave earlier. You need to get out of there." Katie thought her Mom was really sounding worried now.

"It's OK, really. I am leaving in the morning, bright and early. If I get stuck in traffic, I'll have plenty of daylight to get to you. Since Stella stalled earlier, it's really not bad here at the moment. Just really breezy." She could hear muffled words as her mother relayed the information to Katie's father.

Weathering the Storm

"Your father wants to talk to you," Deborah said. Katie had always thought they were excellent as a phone conversation tag team.

"Hey Pumpkin, how's it going?" Although Katie knew her father would be concerned for her well-being, Chester Woodruff had let her know in the past that she had good sense to handle most situations well.

"It's OK Dad. We got delayed at work and I didn't want to start the trip to your house this late at night. I plan on leaving at first light."

"That sounds sensible. Do you have the car gassed up? We're seeing long lines at the gas stations on the news reports from down there."

"The tank's full and I even had the oil changed at the start of hurricane season. The car is running fine."

"Ok Pumpkin. See you tomorrow. Be careful. Here's your mother." Chester passed the phone back to his wife. Although Katie didn't hear a lot of sentimentality coming across the airwaves, she knew her Dad was concerned, and he cared.

"Your father says I shouldn't worry so I'll do my best not to. Give us a call when you leave. We'll have dinner waiting for you when you get here."

"Sounds like a plan. I'll call you in the morning." After trading 'I love yous' with her mother, Katie disconnected the call and put the phone on the counter. Taking a big drink of deliciously cold water, she thought about going into her bedroom to finish packing. Since she was in no hurry to get on the road, Katie picked up her cellphone and sat down at the dinette table. Storm or no storm, she wanted to give Lola an update on her visit to Dr. MacDermitt's office. As her friends had shared their experiences over pink drinks a few days ago, Katie had gained strength from their stories. She wanted to keep them aware of what was happening.

As the sky's color changed through the lace curtains on the kitchen windows, Katie listened to the phone ring. One thing she had to say about this storm, it did produce beautiful sunsets in between cloud bursts.

"Hey," Lola answered after the third ring.

"Hi Lola. How's the traffic?"

"I wouldn't know," Lola said a bit sullenly. "We're still in Rienville. Are you on the road?"

"I'm still here. I thought y'all were leaving this afternoon?"

"Well the car's packed and ready to go. We had a bit of excitement here. A transformer down the street was hit by a dead tree that fell during a gust of wind. Knocked out our power, so we've decided to stay and reassess our options." Katie heard Lola sigh through the phone connection.

"If you have no power, why not leave?" The question sounded logical to Katie when she said it.

"We have meat in the freezer that can handle a few days without power and still be OK. Having it go out even before the storm hits will make things dicey. Any more than 3 days and the meat will start to spoil. It'd be a sin to waste this much game. We are discussing if we want to pack it up or cook it up. We've got the outside grills connected to the natural gas lines in the house. One of the best decisions we ever made."

Katie agreed, and then proceeded to tell her about her visit with the oncologist.

"I've always liked Hill. He's a good guy and has more common sense than most. I'm really glad you have a game plan. You need to give Rose a call and let her know."

"I have already talked with her. She was at the hospital with a sick friend. I saw their truck when I was leaving." Katie shared what details she had, and Lola said she thought the woman was a mutual friend. Lola could spell Rose at the hospital if needed.

"I guess I should finish cleaning up since I'll be leaving early. I hope the freezer dilemma works out for the best."

"No worries." Lola sang 'Happy Trails to you' over the line and signed off.

Weathering the Storm

*

Lola ended the phone and went to check on Rene. Not ready to give up yet, he had hooked up a generator under the lean-to outside the garage and fed a line into the utility room and the freezer.

"I've got enough gas to run it for a few days if we need to. I'm going to keep it hooked up to the freezer until the house gets too hot for us to stand it and then we can connect it to the window unit." Rene yelled as he stood proudly over the noisy machine.

The Normandy family had once spent a week in sweltering heat in the aftermath of a 'little' tropical storm. After that adventure, the family had invested in two window units and the generator. If nothing else, they would have cold storage for food, alternating the power cord from the freezer to the fridge, and two cool rooms for sleeping. Since the kids were away at college, they would only need to cool one bedroom this time around.

Getting a diet soda out of the ice chest in the garage, Lola sat under the back-patio cover. Since it was now dusk and there was a stiff breeze, she actually felt comfortable. She pulled out her cellphone and tapped on Rose's name on the screen. Amazingly, the call went through on the first time.

"I hear you're drinking crappy coffee, sitting in an uncomfortable chair," Lola teased Rose when she answered the phone.

"Either you've been talking to our young friend or your network of spies is better than I thought." Rose took a sip of said lousy coffee. Its lack of warmth did nothing to help the taste.

"Yes, Katie called to let me know about her meeting with Hill. What's going on with you?"

"Long story short is I'm at the hospital with Helena Guici. I went to check on her while Patrick finished getting the dogs ready to go. When I got to her house, I found her unconscious on the floor. Called 911 and they brought her here. I'm staying with her until her daughter can get here from their house in Mississippi. Because of the evacuation traffic on the interstate, she has had to take the backroads to get here and it will still be a while. So now we plan on leaving in the morning."

"Wow. That must have been exciting." Lola grimaced at the thought. "How is she doing? Do they know what happened?"

Rose's patience level was dropping after being in the hospital for several hours. Her voice took on a snarky quality.

"Well, it seems that in this era of patient privacy, I can call 911 and sit by her bedside, But I'm not allowed to actually know what's the matter with her. What I've been able to tell so far is she's seems to be comfortable. They don't know what caused her to be out on the floor and she's awake at times and then she's not. Even though I'm not family, they are letting me stay. When Helena's awake, she gets agitated without someone she knows with her." All snarkiness aside, Rose was concerned.

"I'm sorry you're not on the road, but I'm glad you are there for her. When is her daughter getting there to relieve you?"

"If all goes well, June should be here shortly. When she called last, she was about two hours away by her estimation. It's slow going off the interstate. Why aren't you on the road?" Lola could hear hospital sounds in the background and thought of the people who could not be evacuated.

"A dead tree met a transformer on our street a few hours ago. Rene is now concerned about our stuff in the freezer and is rethinking us going at all. We always plan on the power being out a good three days, but not losing it before it even makes landfall. So, we are sitting tight with the generator running. Everything is ready to go."

"When do you think you'll have power back? You can come stay at our house tonight. Every guest bed comes with a free snuggle dog." It was a long running joke how Rose and Patrick slept in a virtual dog pile each night. Even with the endless complaints of leg cramps and cold feet from the dogs shifting the covers, Lola knew Rose and Patrick weren't content without their pups snuggled with them each night.

"I don't know when they will be able to put up a new transformer. Evidently you can't just throw one of these things up at the drop of a hat. The house is only a little on the warm side so far and we've got a window unit for the bedroom. We'll be good tonight."

"Yeah, you should be ok. The offer still stands. There's always room at the Marino Inn."

"One thing we could use is help with water. Can we come over and fill up our emergency jugs?" Lola kept a dozen empty gallon jugs strung up in the garage for just this type of situation. She usually filled her 'stringer' bottles before the power went out, and with it, their water pump. The blown transformer had messed up that part of her storm prep.

"Of course, bring them by when you can."

The friends chit-chatted for a few more minutes before Lola heard Rene moving things around in the house. She signed off the call, knowing Rose would touch base with Lola in the morning. Finishing up her soda, Lola looked out over the backyard. She took a deep breath. Closing her eyes, she said a prayer for safe travels for her friends and for sanctuary for the people stuck at the hospital.

When Lola opened her eyes, dusk had given way to night. With their power out, the backyard was particularly dark. Stars became visible and then covered by waves of ghost-like clouds. After enjoying the velvety darkness for some time, Lola rose from the chair and went inside to help her husband.

28.6N, 89.6W. 110 MPH. 117 miles south of Rienville.

The next morning, Rose and Patrick loaded the dogs along with a large thermos of coffee and headed toward the interstate on ramp. Stella's rain bands had arrived in earnest after Rose came home from the hospital just before midnight. Between the winds blowing consistently at 20 to 30 miles per hour and the intermittent rain, it was enough to make everything in the car feel damp.

Luckily, although their clothes were more wet than dry, Patrick had been able to get the dogs into the car in between squalls. *At least we won't have the aroma of wet dog with us all the way to Tuscaloosa.* Rose gave thanks for small blessings.

As they got closer to the interstate, traffic began to back up. The slow tempo of the windshield wipers gave Rose and Patrick glimpses of the stop-n-go traffic.

"If we traffic is already this bad…. This does not bode well," Rose murmured.

"Does this seem to be moving a bit slower than usual to you?" Patrick asked as they crawled down the road. Ruby leaned her long red snout over the back of the driver's seat and panted into Patrick's ear. Shushing the dog to back up, the young vizsla finally settled with the other two canines dozing in the car's storage area.

"People in the city must have decided it was a good idea to leave," Rose commented as they inched down the road. Rienville was a major intersection of interstates out of Louisiana. Sort of like the Atlanta airport. *Sometimes it seems like you have to go through here to get anywhere else.*

After another a quarter hour of stop-start traffic, they neared the on-ramp and could see blue lights flashing in the tops of the pine trees up ahead. They crested the last rise before the entrance and looked down the shoulder of the road and around the line of cars ahead of them. Rose could see state trooper cars blocking the interstate entrance. Two troopers in neon yellow slickers with orange light batons stood in the road way, waving people to continue on straight. Every few cars, they would bend down to talk to a driver who had stopped for an explanation.

"This is not good," Patrick said as they creeped forward. "Not good at all."

The couple had been listening to country music on the satellite radio. *Perhaps we should have been listening to the local talk radio station.* Patrick motioned to the radio while keeping his eyes on the car ahead of them. Rose reached over to the console and changed the channel. After several commercials, the announcer came back with

Weathering the Storm

news of the traffic snarls leaving New Orleans, but no details about their section of roadway.

They continued to listen as traffic moved forward. Finally, it was their turn to lower the window and get the official report.

"The interstate is closed until McNeil folks," the officer said before Patrick could even ask. "There's a hazardous waste spill on the roadway just north of Picayune." Rose calculated that meant almost fifty miles of interstate was closed and no use to anyone. An alternative route down the backroads of Mississippi would not be quick.

"How long until they reopen the highway?" With this rain and the traffic, Patrick could use some good news.

"We're estimating six to eight hours, sir. They've got equipment coming from Alexandria. The roads are jammed, and it will be a while for it to get here and do the work." The officer proceeded to suggest alternate highways to take heading north. Patrick was not convinced.

"Me and how many thousand other people?"

Grinning, the trooper took a bandana out of his pocket, took off his hat and wiped the rain from his face.

"That I couldn't say, sir. Your guess is as good as mine." He replaced his hat. "I do need you to move along. Be safe."

Patrick proceeded through the intersection and looked at the long line of cars heading in the opposite direction, knowing they would also be turned away by the troopers as well. He pulled into a Waffle House parking lot. Putting the car in park, he turned off the windshield wipers. The rain immediately made the outside world blur into an impressionist landscape.

Rose had already gotten out the paper atlas from under the seat. GPS and map apps were great for some, but she preferred a paper map to see the big picture without having to squint at a tiny screen.

Opening it to the Mississippi pages, she moved her index finger down to the corner. Luckily, Rienville was located on the small bit of the bayou state printed on the page.

Soon doggie noses appeared over their shoulders, partly from the car being still and probably more from the aroma of bacon coming from the restaurant and through their air conditioning system.

Rose and Patrick plotted multiple routes, using the thin blue lines meandering north. It would take hours to get anywhere in the best of times. With the addition of a multitude of drivers thinking the same, it would make for an extremely long day.

"How bad is the storm right now?" he asked his wife, peering out the windshield as another small squall line passed over them. Patrick grimaced when he realized he was almost shouting to be heard over the hard beat of the rain on the roof of the car.

"Before we left the house, it was still a Two at 110 miles per hour."

"Was it moving?" They had learned from previous experience; a slow-moving tropical storm could create just as much trouble as a fast-moving larger storm.

Rose took out her smart phone and pulled up the National Hurricane Center's latest advisory.

"She's moving now at a good clip. If she doesn't slow down and only grows a little, the storm should be past us in two, maybe three days," so said the family's amateur meteorologist.

"What do you think?" he asked. "Keep heading north or turn around and hunker down for a few days?" Patrick reached up and scratched Gertie Mae's soft ears as she laid her head on his shoulder. A long ride was nothing for the humans in the car, but the dogs would not have a good time, especially Gertie Mae. She was an old girl.

"I think we can tough it out at home. I'd rather be nestled there instead of stuck inside this moving box for the next few days. The congestion on the roads is not going to get better." Rose looked out the side window at the blurred view of the restaurant's sign.

"Then home it will be," said Patrick. He put the car into gear and started to pull out of the parking place. Rose put her hand on his as it rested on the gearshift.

Weathering the Storm

"Hold on. I want to run inside before we start the crawl back home." Patrick slid the car's controls back into park, although he did not turn the engine off. Rose wiggled into her windbreaker, grabbed her wallet and dove out of the car. Ruby took the opportunity to jump into the front seat and fogged up the windows on that side of the car.

A few minutes later, Patrick turned the car around at the back of the parking lot and moved it to outside the restaurant's door. Rose ran through the rain with two to-go cups in her hands.

It took them some time to exit the lot and get into the long line of cars heading back toward Rienville. As they got to the troopers, Patrick rolled down his window and Rose handed him the cups of sweet iced tea she had purchased during her pit stop.

"You guys stay safe out here," Patrick told him, as he handed the officers the Styrofoam cups.

"Thanks so much." The trooper walked the few steps to pass the second cup to other officer, the one who gave Patrick the bad news earlier. That man waved his thanks to the couple and popped the lid for a long drink. Even with the cool rain, Rose knew they were both sweating under their slickers in the tropical humidity that came with storms like this one.

Patrick rolled up the window and moved through the intersection, headed for home. The dogs did not settle back down as he picked up speed. Rose wondered if their buddies in the backseat sensed the car was heading for home. As uncomfortable as hurricanes could make life, Rose was good with their decision to return home and was looking forward to getting out of the car.

*

As Rose and Patrick navigated the traffic snarl, rain splattered Katie's living room window. She listened to the local traffic report and looked at the animated road maps on the television. None of the news

109

was good. Evidently, the interstate she had planned on taking north was closed indefinitely and alternate routes were being recommended. None of the state highways sounded familiar to Katie.

Getting to Nashville is not going to be easy.

She picked up the land line and called Lola's home number. Cellphones were proving useless for calling. Texting was still available.

"Hey. Sorry for calling so early. I had hoped you'd still be home."

"No problem. Are you on the road?" Lola cradled the receiver in the crook of her shoulder as she cleaned the kitchen.

"No and that's why I'm calling. I checked the news before I got in the car and the interstate going toward Nashville is closed due to a bad accident or something. Can you or Rene recommend an alternative route?"

"That's not good. Hold on a minute," Katie heard Lola relay the information to her husband and a brief discussion ensued between the two before Lola came back on the line.

"Rene said your best bets would be the highways through Kiln or Sun, depending on where the blockage is on the interstate. Unfortunately, they will also take you way out of the way before you can get back on I-59."

"That's what I was afraid of. I'm not sure what to do at this point. Channel 4 says the storm should make landfall tomorrow morning."

"You really don't want to get stuck on the road when the winds start whipping up. Hold on again." The conversation coming over the phone sounded muffled, as Lola covered the receiver. After a moment, her friend came back on the line.

"Katie, since the roads are probably jammed by now, it's probably safer for you to not head to Nashville. Why don't you come stay at our house for the duration? We've got the room, plenty of food and it's pretty comfortable even with our lack of central air conditioning."

"I don't know. My parents are pretty worried about me going through my first hurricane by myself." Katie frowned at the television screen. On location reporters wearing rain gear were sharing their observations about the wreck that was blocking her path to her parent's house. It looked bad.

Weathering the Storm

"Believe me; we don't like to stay for storms ourselves. This time, though, I don't think it would be prudent to try and get on the road. When you take the state highways, even in perfect weather, it can take hours extra to get anywhere when conditions are good. If you leave now and can't make it all the way to your parent's house, there won't be a motel room to be had so you'll have to stay in your car. That would not be wise."

Katie looked out the window, streaked from the rain and screwed up her nose. What a mess.

"You can tell your folks our house makes a great sanctuary. We're surrounded by hardwoods that fair pretty well in the wind and we're several feet above the usual flood levels. If our house takes water, the rest of the city has bigger problems to deal with. Lola truly believed that last statement.

Realizing the crash on the interstate had really already been made the decision for her, she queried her soon to be hostess.

"If you're sure it would be no problem for me to stay?"

"Absolutely. The kids are away at school and we have told them not to come home. If we do have issues, an extra set of hands could come in handy," Lola walked around the kitchen as she continued to empty the dishwasher.

"Ok. I really appreciate this. Let me give my parents a call to let them know I'm staying put and then I'll be over. What can I bring?" Katie scanned her cozy kitchen.

"If you want, bring anything that won't last a day or two in the frig if the power cuts off. That would be fine," said Lola. Katie heard Rene talking from across the room.

"Rene says if you have any ice in the freezer, it would be welcome."

"That I can do. See you soon," Katie finished the call and headed for the storage room for her small cooler. Quietly, she formatted her call to her parents. Katie knew she had to sound positive without relaying

111

to them how totally unconfident she was in her decision to stay. They just didn't have to know that.

*

Rose and Patrick pulled into their driveway 11 miles and two hours after they had left. The dogs in the back were eager to get out of the car, even though the rain was coming down in torrents at the moment.

"Open the garage door and we'll make a run for it." Rose yelled, over the barks and whines coming from their canines. She pulled the hood from her raincoat over her salt-n-pepper hair. It was a wonder Patrick could hear her above the cacophony from the back of the car. Their overgrown pups wanted out and they wanted it now.

As the large door slowly rose up into the ceiling, Patrick turned off the motor and grabbed his eye glasses from the cozy in the roof of the car.

"On the count of three. One. two." He opened his door and a doggie tsunami rushed over the seats and Rose's shoulder as they barreled out and ran for the house. After the third dog used the side of her seat as a launch pad, Rose left the car and followed the parade into the garage, slamming her car door on the way.

"What happened to three?" she asked, shaking the rain off her coat, much like their band of mutts were doing onto the garage floor.

"You snooze, you lose," Patrick looked like an imp as he smiled at Rose, rainwater dripping from the bill of his hat.

*

Katie arrived at Lola's house during a break in the rain. Parking in the extra side slot usually reserved for the kid's car, she stopped to take a deep breath and gave thanks for a welcoming place to weather this storm.

Grabbing her purse and a small Igloo cooler, she opened the car door. Katie was greeted by the delicious smells of a barbeque grill at work and the jarring sound of a gas generator. Rounding the car, Katie saw the generator situated under a lean-to about ten feet from the side of the house. A thick orange extension cord ran from the machine to the garage. She gingerly stepped over it, not wanting to harm what could be an important part of allowing her a comfortable night's sleep in the coming days. To the side of the noisy machine was an assortment of red gasoline containers.

I wonder how long that will last, Katie mused as she walked by.

As she followed her nose, Katie made her way to the backyard. With all the rain making the ground a quagmire, she was thankful for the spiffy rubber boots Rose had teased her into buying a few months ago. They had gone to get Katie some footwear for the coming storm season. As she walked toward the utilitarian black rubber boots, Rose informed her that no self-respecting Louisiana woman would wear those unless they were blinged out with gold fleur de lies. Moving over a few aisles, they found a selection of colorful waterproof boots in various decorative patterns.

The bright orange and blue plaid pair spoke to Katie. Rose had laughed and said you could take the girl out of Tennessee, but not the school spirit out of the girl. *You got that right*, Katie thought as she clutched the boots to her chest on the way to the checkout counter. The boots would match her favorite baseball cap.

Katie rounded the corner of the house. An arbor covered with honeysuckle vines created a canopy of sweet-smelling flowers and blessed shade over the patio. Even with the breeze, the temperature was warm enough for Katie to feel small beads of sweat roll down her back. The tinny sounds of a banjo wafted over the back yard and she could hear Rene singing along to 'Blue Moon of Kentucky'. Amazingly, she recognized the old recording and the singer as the daughter of Ruby and Hubert Davis from her own Music City. Hubert Davis and the Season Travelers were a group her parents took her to see on a regular basis during her high school days. She had even had a few dates at their venue, the Wind in the Willows.

Rene didn't sound too bad. Katie started humming along. Bluegrass music always made her think of home.

Rene looked up when Katie started walking through the grass.

"Welcome." He called over his shoulder toward the open kitchen window. "Lola, Katie's here." As curtains moved in the breeze, Katie could see Lola working at the sink.

"That smells delicious. Do you always eat this well while battling nature?" She took a seat in a wicker lawn chair upwind from the smoke coming from the grill. A larger smoker was off a bit in the yard, bellowing out its own drifts of sweet-scented fumes into the branches of a swaying maple tree.

"We didn't do such a good job this year emptying out the chest freezer before hurricane season started. Since we have to hunker down this time around, we need to cook up the meat in there. Hope you're hungry," Rene said smiling as he turned over a large roast on the grill. It was located at the far end of the patio, so the heat rose outside the patio's flowering cover.

Katie looked at the size of the smoker and the amount of meat on the grill. *When is the army arriving because Rene has enough food to feed them all?*

"This is one of the times I enjoy having a grill attached to the house line." He closed the lid on the large stainless-steel cooker. "Gas still flows even with the power off and I don't have to go find charcoal." He reached for the bottle of water on the patio table and took a long swig. Pointing it at Katie, he gave the standard non-verbal request of 'want one?' "We've got beer and soda in the green cooler."

"Thanks." Katie moved to the antique cooler on the end of patio. Picking out a bottle of soda, she took off the cap with the opener attached to the cooler's side. The first swig was ice cold and offered perfect relief from the heat.

"Seriously though, how much meat are you cooking?"

Rene took another drink and put the bottle down before picking up the lid on the grill. As he hummed along with the music bringing to mind her hometown, he carefully pulled the roast off the heat and on to a large wooden cutting board lined with aluminum foil. He quickly wrapped the meat and placed it in one of the two plastic coolers nearby. 'Normandy' was painted in big, black letters across the top of each white lid.

Pointing at the smoker, Rene gave her a rundown on what was cooking at the moment. The smoker was filled with fowl; ducks and a small turkey. The grill had hosted four boar roasts and they were just finishing up.

"On the few occasions we have stayed for a storm, I have cooked up a few things and took them over to the police department and our local fire hall. Most of those guys," Rene paused and grinned at Katie, "and ladies, have sent their families off to safer places and can't leave their posts. They sleep on cots and eat those nasty MREs for the duration. Lola cooks up something for the side dish and I take over a cooler of roast or ribs or whatever we have in the freezer. At least they can eat well." He took another sip of water as he sat down. "Since we've lost power even before the storm made landfall, Lola and I decided last night to cook up everything. It won't go to waste."

Lola walked out onto the patio, wiping her hands on a dish towel. She wore an apron that said, 'Everything's Better with Butter'. Lola looked like she'd been busy in the kitchen. Her brown hair was up in a messy pony tail and the heat was causing curls to escape from the rubber band. She gave Katie a smile and bent over to give her friend a quick hug.

"I'm glad you decided to join us. Even without power, it's better than being by yourself for your first storm. Did you get a hold of your parents?"

Katie nodded with a slight grimace as she took another sip of beer.

"They didn't take it very well, but what can I do. I told them what you said about being stuck on backroads when the storm made landfall. That seemed to help. They are still worried."

Lola grabbed a hard cider and a bottle of water out of the cooler and sat down in one of the wicker chairs. When she blew out a sigh, her bangs puffed up on her forehead.

"I can understand how she feels. If either Roslyn or Rey were stuck in the path of a storm, I'd be a mess," she said taking a sip. To add effect to her words, the wind chose to rise at that moment and rain started to fall. Where they were sitting closest to the house, it was dry. Patrick, back at the grill, was getting the occasional rain drop while checking the temperature in the center of another roast before taking it off the fire.

Looking up, Katie tried to see why the rain seemed to be targeting Rene. All she could see was vines and flowers. Lola noticed the way Katie was looking back and forth.

"There's a piece of plastic on top of the arbor that extends a few feet from the house. We wanted to be able to sit out here in the rain but covering the entire roof made it too hot because the breeze could not get through." Lola took turns sipping her cider and drinking from the bottle of water. "This way, we have the shade from the vines and can still sit outside and listen to the rain without feeling it. At least for some of us," she said, grinning at her husband as more raindrops found their way onto Rene while he worked. The scent of honeysuckle perfumed the air.

"Cool." Katie sat back and listened to the rain. They silently watched Rene as he removed the last of the grilled roasts and prepared them for the cooler. Going into the house, he returned with a pan of raw meat. These pieces were larger than the ones he just finished cooking. They were also swimming in a marinade of spices.

"Elk", Rene said as he placed them on the grill and adjusted the flames to a lower level. He left the pan on the side and covered it with a piece of aluminum foil. Seeing Katie's questioning gaze, he offered an explanation. "As I turn them, I give them a good dose of marinade to keep them from drying out."

"Sounds good. I've never had elk or boar. Does it taste gamey?"

"Not the way Rene cooks them. He's a pro, literally. He's got ribbons for his boar roast recipe from the wild game cook-off." Lola

Weathering the Storm

beamed at her husband's back. Katie could tell he appreciated the praise by his stance as he worked at the grill.

"Then I look forward to tasting the work of a master."

Putting the last roast in the cooler, he turned to Lola.

"Is the rest of the food ready?"

Getting up from her chair, Lola started for the kitchen. Katie picked up her empty bottle and her small cooler and followed her. Rene lifted the cooler and joined the parade through the kitchen door.

The kitchen smelled almost as good as the outside, with the aromas of baking and home.

"You can put one of the roasts in the crock and then into the oven. I've got it on warm," said Lola, as she opened the gas oven door. She pulled out a pan of baked macaroni and cheese and set it on the stove top. Rene lifted the ceramic dish into the oven and closed the door.

Covering the casserole with aluminum foil, she turned to the other counter. Taking a dish towel off the top of a pan of peach cobbler, she covered it with foil as well.

"I used up the milk and the shredded cheese in the one and the pie crust and the peaches from the freezer for the other." Rene raised the lid on the container and his wife stacked them on top of the meat.

"Where do you want me to put the things I brought from home?" Katie asked, lifting her small cooler to the counter and opened it. "There's not much, just some juice, fruit and veggies."

"Put the juice in the frig since we have it hooked up to the generator," said Lola, looking over her friend's shoulder. "The apples can stay on the counter and I'll use those vegetables for dinner. Just leave them here."

"You ladies want to come with me to the station?" Rene asked as he lugged the heavy container to the front door.

"I want to finish taking stock of what still needs to be cooked and I'll get the ribs ready for the smoker. Katie, why don't you go? You can see the command center and get a feel for what the city has to do during times like this."

"I don't want to get in the way," Katie answered, looking from one friend to the other.

"You won't be in the way. Plus, your smiling face and home cooked food will raise their spirits. They have a long few days ahead of them." Lola said. A gust of hard rain rattled against the living room window. All three looked out and saw the water coming down hard.

"It figures my rain coat is in my car." Katie knew she'd be drenched by the time she made it to her Toyota.

"Here's one of mine. It's a little big, but it will keep you dry." Lola pulled a Cubbie's blue rain slicker from the coat hook in the front hall. "Take my keys and you can open the hatch for Rene." she unclipped the keys from her purse. Rene had already put on his OD green wind breaker.

Lola reached up on her toes and gave her husband a buzz on his check. Rene's face bore an exaggerated grimace as she kissed him, then broke out in a grin. He winked at Katie.

"Be safe out there. There's still no word from Dad. See if anyone there can tell you about the roads into his place please," Lola said as she reached for the door knob.

"Ok, let's go." Rene hefted the heavy box waist high. He motioned for his wife to open the door. As he stepped out, Katie clicked the key fob and saw the lights on the car signal it was unlocked.

"Uggggghhh!" Rene yelled as he plunged into the rain. Katie followed, splashing through the water on the driveway. She reached the SUV a step behind him. Reaching around, she opened the hatchback for him and then ran to the passenger side door. She jumped in and shut the door quickly. Rene followed a moment after. As they pressed the hoods of their jackets down and shook the rain off their faces, they were both laughing. Katie could see Lola still standing in the front doorway, laughing as well.

"Does yelling help you run faster?" Katie asked as Rene started the car.

Weathering the Storm

"No," he said. "It just makes it more exciting." He grinned as he backed out of the driveway.

*

As they drove toward the Rienville's city center, Katie could now truly imagine what a ghost town would look like. Only a scattering of cars were on the road between Lola's house and the police station in the older part of town. Although it had been pouring when they left the house, they were in between rain bands again and Rene' could turn off the windshield wipers.

Tree branches, pine cones and scraps of paper were toss across the road as they headed downtown. Rain or no rain, the wind seemed constant with gusts that shook the car. *Stella must be getting closer.* Katie continued to gaze out the car window. The lack of people was eerie. *I guess it's almost time to meet the old girl.*

Pulling up in front of city's municipal buildings, Rene' put on his hazard lights.

"Help me carry the cooler to the front door and then you can stay with it while I park the car." They got out of the SUV and moved to the back of the vehicle. Looking around while the tailgate slowly lifted, she wondered about just how many people were working in such nasty weather. There were a lot of police cars, odd trucks and a few military-looking vehicles parked in front of the building.

Each grabbing a cooler handle, they moved in tandem to the wall next to the front door and placed it along the side. Katie took a seat on the cooler and waited while Rene took off to find a parking spot.

Hopefully it won't be raining when it's time to leave. She looked up at the clouds moving across the sky like ropes of cotton candy. The clanging flag hook on the city hall flagpole beat out a metallic tattoo.

As she was sky watching, the door opened and a policeman in raingear exited. Noticing her sitting on the cooler, he stopped.

"Can I help you?" the officer asked. He looked closely at Katie.

She stood up and turned toward the door. He looked familiar and it took her a moment to remember him as the guy that helped her fill her sand bags. Her mind went blank. *Why am I always so bad with remembering names?*

"I'm waiting on my friend. We're delivering some dinner for the staff here. He's parking the car." Katie waved a hand down the street. Their helper from the sand pile looked different in the blue uniform and neon yellow slicker. The navy blue RPD baseball cap he wore had flipped the switch in Katie's mind as to who he was. She always had a weakness for guys in ball caps.

Katie glanced at his chest, trying to catch the name badge, but just the edge of the plate was visible. As she looked up, the hood of Lola's rain jacket fell away.

Jake has also been at a loss until he saw her hat. That's when he had realized she was the woman from the sand bag station. Her name was on the tip of his tongue. It was a family name, he thought, and he quickly went through a list in his mind. Katherine felt close.

"It's Katie, isn't it?" Jake asked as he held out his hand. Clasping it, Katie gave it a shake and nodded an affirmative.

"You're right. Katie Woodruff," she said as she slowly let go of his fingers. "You helped us at the sandbag station." *Please offer your name.* She was at an embarrassing loss. They both shifted closer to the wall as the rain had started again. They moved deeper under the overhang from second floor landing.

Flicking his jacket open to put his hands in his pocket, she glimpsed his nametag – Mesch, J. *Jake. His name is Jake.*

"Jake, right?" When he nodded, she asked. ""I thought you were an AC guy?"

"I am. That's my day job that pays the bills. I'm a reserve officer with the Rienville Police Department." She wasn't being whimsical when she thought he seemed to stand a bit taller.

"I'm not familiar with the term. What's a reserve officer?" A burst of wind blew the side of her hair into her face. She moved it back behind her ear and pulled the hood closer around her neck.

Weathering the Storm

"It's a volunteer position. We get the same training and certification as the full-time officers. We commit to voluntarily work so many hours a month. Many of my shifts are during festivals, Mardi Gras and special events. Everyone is called in during emergencies like this."

"Sounds like a lot of effort for little reward."

"Well, we get fed well by some very kind people if the food in that cooler is as good as it smells." Jake leaned toward the box and took a deep breath.

As if on cue, a dark green blur came down the street through the rain and onto the porch. Shaking like a mongrel dog, Rene shook off the water weighing him down and flipped back the hood on his jacket.

"Hey," he said and held out his right hand to Jake. "Rene Normandy. We're here to deliver some comfort food for the boys in blue. I guess that includes you. Is Chief Poirer inside?" The men shook hands.

"Nice to meet you. I'm Jake Mesch. The chief's in the EOC on the second floor. Whatever is in there smells great. Need some help carrying it in?" asked the officer.

"I'm sure Katie would appreciate it if you took the other handle. Who would have thought boar roast and homemade macaroni and cheese could weigh this much." Rene grabbed one handle. Jake was smiling when he lifted his end and turned toward the door. Katie opened the glass door with the thin sheet of plywood covering most of it and held it while the men carried the provisions through. They headed up the stairs.

"They're using the city council conference room as a temporary dining hall. There's a small kitchen with a frig and microwave connected to it. You can put the food in there. Once its put away, I'll take you to the chief," Jake said as he led the way down the hall.

As they entered the conference room, they saw two people eating po-boys at the long, wooden table. The diners waved and continued their quiet conversation while the three moved down the side of the room and entered the kitchen.

A woman, who looked to be in her mid-50s, was working inside. Wearing a Saints t-shirt and an RPD ball cap over her light brown hair, she was putting paper plates and a container filled with plastic forks on the counter. Hearing someone walk in, she turned and greeted them with a smile.

"What have we got here?" she asked as Rene and Jake placed the cooler next to the counter. Putting out his hand, Rene introduced himself and Katie to the woman.

"I'm Terry Poirer, Craig's wife. It's nice to meet you," She shook hands with Rene and Katie. "I'm the chief cook and bottle washer for the duration. Something smells delicious."

"My wife Lola and I thought you might be able to use some comfort food during the siege. We cooked up a few boar roasts and some smoked turkey. Lola also made up a tray of mac and cheese and her famous peach cobbler." Rene lifted the lid to show Terry. A variety of wonderful aromas permeated the small kitchen.

"Looks like we'll be eating like kings and queens. Thanks for thinking of us. If you don't mind us keeping the cooler for a day, I'll leave it all inside it until supper time and serve it then. We don't have an oven, just a microwave, and I know it will stay hot in there," Terry said.

"No problem. Keep it as long as you need. It's got our name on the top," said Rene. "Let me leave my number and if you need more, just let us know. We're cooking up our freezer and will have plenty to share." Rene wrote his cell number on a dry erase board on the frig.

"We really appreciate this. The guys never go hungry during one of these events, but real food is always preferable to the emergency meals FEMA passes on to us. Please tell Lola thanks from us. I've met her at a fund raiser not too long ago."

She turned to Katie. "I don't think we've met before. I don't know any Woodruffs."

"I've only lived here for about a year."

Weathering the Storm

"This is her first storm," Rene said, putting the marker back on the shelf.

"Well, let's hope Stella is kind to us all and moves down the road quickly," the chief's wife commented as they all walked toward the door to the hall.

Jake moved forward and motioned down the hall.

"I thought I'd show them the command center before they headed out. They can see where their tax dollars go."

"Great idea Jake. It's nothing fancy, but it does lend an air of authority to the place. Safe days ahead to you both." The temporary kitchen manager turned back to her domain.

"We've got the EOC, or Emergency Operations Center, set up in the council chambers. They coordinate the police, fire and parish emergency services personnel from a central location during storms or disasters." Jake made his way to the end of the hall and opened a double door.

Greeting the trio was a room full of computer monitors and a dozen people, most of them on the phone. The overall sound coming from the room was a low hum. It reminded Katie of the sound she once heard when she visited a friend's apiary. Clashing with the many voices was the drum of rain against the room's wall of windows. *The view of Olde Rienville is probably lovely on regular days.* Today, it was just a gray landscape mottled by the rain.

Taking up most of one wall was a huge map of the parish with notes stuck to it at specific points.

"How are things going so far," Rene asked Jake as they looked over the map. Katie had an idea of where her home was and also where Rose and Lola's houses were located. There were no notes near those points, which she took as good news. Most of them seemed to be posted along the coastline.

"We've gotten a few calls on the south side of town from people worried about the water rising in the streets. It looks like Stella will come in tomorrow at high tide. That's never a good thing. They really need to evacuate now." Jake tilted his head to listen to a call coming over the radio clipped to his shoulder. They heard a set of numbers relayed over the speaker. It didn't appear that the message was for him and Jake turned back to them.

"Any word from the Bayou Oiseaux area?" Rene asked, looking over that section of the map.

"Last I heard, the water was up to the highway, but not over the roadway yet. Do you have someone out there?" asked Jake.

"Lola's Dad lives in a raised camp on the bayou. He's a tough old bird and we couldn't get him to come into town. Sounds like he's staying put for now."

"If his place is up, and the winds stay as expected, he should be okay." Jake leaned his head over his shoulder again to hear another message over his radio.

"We need to get out of your hair and back home before the real rain starts. Looking at the radar screen over there, we've got about an hour before it becomes a real downpour." Rene turned to offer his hand to the officer.

"Stay safe out there," he said as they clasped hands and broke apart.

"You all as well." Jake turned toward Katie.

"Hope your first storm is quick and boring. Let me know if you need help with any clean-up afterwards. Still have my card?" He gave her a warm smile.

"I do, thanks. You take care too." They left Jake in the EOC and made their way down the steps to the front door. Katie buttoned Lola's rain jacket and put the hood up as they opened the door.

"Remember, yelling helps," said Rene as he ran into the rain, screeching like a banshee. A much quieter Katie raced after him. Once again, she gave thanks for her boots as she ran through the ankle-deep water now covering the street.

*

Weathering the Storm

Patrick walked into the kitchen through the back door and shrugged out of his drenched drover's coat. His wide brim hunting hat had kept the very top of his head dry, but not much else. Looking out the window, Rose could see the sky was darkening earlier than the hour warranted.

"It's coming down sideways now. What's the latest report?" Patrick asked his wife as he hung up the wet items on hooks next to the door. Three noses came over to give him a sniff and to see if he had by chance brought in a selection of snacks. When no such treats appeared, the dogs sauntered back to their respective beds. Patrick did gift each with a conciliatory ear rub.

"I just got the latest coordinates from the radio. They are now saying the eye will pass over Cocodrie about noon tomorrow. We're going to get the brunt of the storm. The good news is she's weakened a bit and is only a little over one hundred miles an hour." Rose finished marking the laminated hurricane map she kept updated on the breakfast bar.

"At least it's moving, and we'll be finished with her soon. I've got everything outside taken care of and the coolers in the garage are ready with ice if we need them."

"Bath tub is filled to flush the toilets and candles and flashlights are ready." Rose gave Patrick a little salute. "You know what that means?" She said grinning.

"Wine time?" Patrick looked hopefully.

"You got it. I've got the pasta ready and the garlic bread in the oven. Go grab a bottle." Rose had spent the afternoon cooking. They would enjoy the fruits of their electric stove and air conditioning for as long as it lasted.

"Maybe I should triage a few extra on the counter in case we lose power and we can't read the labels." Patrick's voice had a teasing tone.

"You're the boy scout in the family. Be prepared." Rose watched him select three bottles from his extensive wine rack. The bottles were marked with labels from his personal cataloging system for rating wine.

"Are those double red stars I see?" Rose looked over his shoulder as he opened the first bottle. Red stars were his top choices and double stars meant for special occasions only.

"If you can't drink the good stuff when facing a possible disaster, when can you?" Under Patrick's hand, the cork left the bottle with a satisfactory 'pop'.

"True, very true." Rose held out two of the lead crystal glasses they saved for special days. Patrick looked appreciatively at the ruby colored liquid as it flowed into the glasses.

"To challenging days," he said.

"To Stella," Rose said, as they gently clinked their glasses together.

*

Katie and Rene retraced their route back to the house. The wipers tried to keep up with the water hitting the windshield with little success. The car's radio was turned to the local news channel where one of the station's meteorologists was giving the latest info on Stella.

"I can't believe this rain." Katie looked out her side window as they passed her office building. It looked abandoned in the descending darkness. Katie checked the car's clock. It was already late afternoon.

"Get used to it." Rene concentrated on avoiding the deep-water pooling in the outer lanes. "It will be like this, or worse, until after Stella passes through. She's a category 2 at the moment and may not weaken much until she travels over land. So far, she seems to be moving at a good clip so that we should only have a few days of this."

"Days?"

"From looking at the radar at the EOC, we're going to be on the east side of the storm. That means we'll get the brunt of it. As the eye makes landfall southwest of us, we'll continue to get the rain on the back end of the storm. It will take a day or two to move through."

Weathering the Storm

"Are you worried about the house flooding?" Katie asked as they passed two police cars sitting driver's side to driver's side in the hospital parking lot.

"Not really. Everyone should worry a little about that because of where we live. Lola and I picked this house partly on the elevation of the neighborhood. We're on a ridge that's about 14 feet above sea level. Her Dad calls it 'Mount Rienville' as it's one of the highest points in town. We didn't take water in Katrina, but it was close. I'm more worried about the trees." Rene finished as he turned into his neighborhood.

The tall pines lined up between many of the houses in the neighborhood swayed in the wind as they drove down the street. They did not have the gentle movement that came with a normal summer rain, but more of an erratic jerking motion. They reminded Katie of performers at a modern dance recital.

"We don't have to be concerned too much with the hardwoods. Their root systems are spread out. It's the pines that can cause the most trouble. When one of those big puppies comes through the roof, it's like a hot knife slicing through butter." Rene passed the fire-blackened pine at the entrance of their street. It stood as a silent sentinel to the power of a falling tree.

Katie's eyes widen when she looked up the street and realized how many pine trees towered over Lola's house. She passed a worried look to Rene as he turned off the car engine in the driveway. The loud drone of the generator penetrated the inside of the car.

"I'm not that concerned about these trees. We lost a lot of the single trees in Katrina and what's left are pines grouped together. I have an arborist friend who told me the ones in groups cut the wind for each other and are less likely to be felled by a strong wind. I know a lot of people panicked after Katrina and took out all their pines. The trouble with that is they drink up an incredible about of water. Since it seems to rain almost daily around here, their yards are pretty spongy.

I'd rather have the trees." Rene zipped up his jacket and opened his door.

Katie looked at the swaying trees towering over the house for a moment before leaving the car. *It is what it is.* She made her way to the front door.

Inside the house, the temperature was warm. Katie thought it was still fairly comfortable. Although the air was damp and heavy, the breeze coming through the partially opened windows did help.

"How were things at city hall?" Lola greeted them at the kitchen doorway, wiping her hands on a dish towel.

"Good." Rene started to take off his rain gear and thought better of it. "We met the Chief's wife Terry at the police station. She says hello to you and thanks for the meal. I'd better check on the grill." He moved though the kitchen and out the backdoor. The others followed his trail of watery drips, with Katie stopping to remove her coat and hang it on the back of a chair, before following outside.

"I checked on grill about 20 minutes ago and everything was fine." Lola reached into a cooler for another hard cider and motioned for Katie to help herself to something to drink.

"That's for the professionals to decide." Rene gave his wife a wink and moved to open the grill. Turning the roasts over, they met with his approval and he lowered the lid, placing the barbeque tongs on the attached table. After checking the temperature on the smoker, he turned back to the women.

"Are the ribs ready to go?" He reached into the ice for a cold beer. Popping the cap using a multi-tool from his pocket, he took a long swing of his favorite craft brew.

"They are marinating in the refrigerator." Lola moved to the edge of the overhang, where the water was dripping through the honeysuckle. Looking over the back yard, she was happy they had been able to cut the grass last week. The standing water in the far back would make using a mower a near impossibility for a week or two. The center of the storm with its expected rainfall, hadn't even arrived yet.

"Once you put the ribs in the smoker, we can move the electrical cords to the window units. The freezer's empty." Lola savored her drink. A gust of wind blew a dead limb from the hickory tree at the back of the lot, narrowly missing the cement bird bath. Dusk was falling fast and very early.

"I don't know about you guys, but I'm hungry. Let's eat." Lola got up and entered the kitchen. Katie followed her into the house.

"What can I help you with?" Katie put her beer on the counter. With the windows open and the air conditioner off, there was a thin layer of moisture on the counter top. *This might be what it feels like to live in a rain forest.*

"I made a cucumber and tomato salad with a few of the things you brought over. We've also got the mac and cheese I made when I did the tray for the police station. You can choose grilled boar or smoked duck or both." Lola moved to open one of the coolers.

"I've never had wild boar, so I think I'd like to try it." Katie washed her hands using one of the gallon water jugs sitting by the sink. "Do you want to use the paper plates on the counter or regular?" she asked as she dried her hands on a dish towel hanging from the oven handle.

"We'll use paper for the duration I think," said her hostess, removing an aluminum covered bundle from the cooler and placing it on a platter. Unwrapping the darkened roast, Lola removed a carving knife and fork from the butcher block on the counter and moved to the kitchen table.

"Since the rain is not crazy yet, let's eat on the patio table. We'll be stuck in the house long enough starting tonight." Opening the back door, Lola reached over for the platter and moved outside. Katie followed with the plates and some plastic silverware.

"About time I get to enjoy the fruit of my labors." Rene turned away from the grill and sat at the table.

Lola returned inside the house to retrieve the side dishes and a roll of paper towels. Setting them in the center of the table, she reached over and squeezed Rene's shoulder.

"And an excellent labor it is and will continue to be this evening. You're in the home stretch."

The three proceeded to load up their plates. As Katie took her first bite of the meat, she became aware of two sets of eyes glancing her way.

"What do you think?" Rene asked before he took a big bite of the wild game. He expressed an appreciative sigh as a smile spread across his face.

"It's surprisingly good. If I didn't know better, I'd say it was a really lean pork loin." Katie took another bite.

"Wild boar is lean because they feed on grass. The meat doesn't have the additives and antibiotics farmers have to use to maintain a healthy herd." Rene moved another chunk of wild pig from the platter to his plate. "Hunting also helps the marsh areas a lot. These animals breed so frequently, and they love to eat marsh grass roots. That in turn messes up the levies."

As they ate, Rene shared his observations from the emergency command center with Lola.

"I asked about James' area. They said the water was up to the road with no real problems so far."

Lola pushed her food around her plate as she looked on the rain coming down outside the cozy enclosure. She had tried to reach her Dad on both his home phone and his cellphone without luck while Rene and Katie were downtown. She shared that news with her companions.

"He's a tough bird, Lola. He knows his limits. Whether we agree with him or not, we need to have faith in his decision-making." Rene concentrated on enjoying the food in front of him and the peaceful sound of rain outside their cozy shelter.

"I know. I just wish I could reach him."

The conversation moved on to the upcoming LSU-Alabama football matchup as the sun set and the rain droned on.

28.8N, 90.0W. 100 MPH. 103 miles south of Rienville.

Rose looked at her laminated hurricane tracking chart sitting on the kitchen counter and carefully put another dot, then drew a line to connect it with the rest of Stella's track. Now the sluggish hurricane would be making landfall west of Houma sometime in the night, with the eye currently sitting less than a hundred miles southwest of New Orleans.

She'll land with the force of a weak Category 2, Rose thought, as she sipped her drink. Looking out the back window, she could see their pack of dogs running through the standing water, already dog-ankle deep in the backyard. Yes, the dogs were a mess and she had pretty much given up mopping the kitchen floor for now. The mess aside, she enjoyed watching them as they joyfully raced each other during the brief lull in the rain.

Rose smiled as she watched them. *Oh, to be a dog sometimes.*

The light streaming through the windows slowly dimmed and the wind picked up its tempo. Rose sensed a change in the weather. The dogs, one by one, stopped running and put their noses in the air, sniffing and snorting. Collectively, they headed for the doggie door at the back of the house as the rain started to fall again.

Rose got up, selected a beach towel from the stack by the back door and moved to intercept her four-legged friends as they entered the doggie door. The dogs brought the swampy smell of damp and mud inside with them. She would be thankful when the rains finally passed.

As Rose attempted to dry a wiggling mass of fur and energy, Stella continued to meander along the coast on her stroll toward land.

*

The kids were safe. Lola had walked down the hall to Rene's office to let him know. They had texted her upon their arrival at their great-uncle's farm located in a parish north of Baton Rouge. He had looked up from his paperwork and, over the top of his half glasses, acknowledged the news. Rene couldn't resist the opportunity to smile at her as he reminded Lola, they were smart, resourceful people who took after their father. Her husband had had no doubt they would heed their parents' warning to get off the campus and move a little further north.

When the track showed Stella strolling further west, the university wisely decided to cancel classes for two days and had strongly suggested evacuation to those students who had a better place to go. The decision had come, early enough to get many on the roads before the traffic was too bad. The administration wasn't stupid, Lola had thought. No one needed thousands of students on campus with no power or running water. The ones who truly couldn't leave would be cared for as they sheltered in place.

After classes were officially cancelled, Rene had called his Uncle Jeb at the family farm and requested sanctuary for his children. His uncle had chided Rene. The old man pretended to be offended that Rene had even had to ask and told him to send Rey and Roslyn on up. Jokingly, he told his nephew he could use the kid's help mucking out the barn. Rene thought his uncle was probably kidding about putting the kids to work. But Rey and Roz would enjoy helping on the farm before the rain reached that far north. Then Rene guessed they would all settle down in the big country kitchen to hear stories from the family archives as the remnants of the storm passed by the farm.

'Arrived. Uncle Jedidiah says hey. Going out to ride Rosie. Stay safe," was Roslyn's text message to her mom. Lola loved that their daughter was one of the few in the family who could spell her great-uncle's name correctly. Rosie the mule was Roslyn's namesake and Lola knew they would enjoy spending time riding through the soybean fields.

With their children safely tucked away at the farm, Lola's thoughts turned again to her dad and the camp on the bayou. The roads to his home were now impassable to everyday vehicles. There wasn't much more that she could do and doing nothing frustrated the hell out of her.

While she had daylight, Lola picked up her wooden hoop and continued to make tiny stitches on a quilt square made up of fabrics of mossy greens and browns. The colors reminded her of the bayou. As she stitched, Lola prayed for her father's safety, Ms. Beryl and anyone else who came to mind. Lola often found quilting and prayer were good for calming the soul.

28.8N, 90.5W. 100 MPH. 101 miles south of Rienville.

Another dot on the map. Rose capped her green sharpie, the one that had been marking Stella's progress since entering the Gulf of Mexico and looked out the darkened kitchen window. With most of their neighbors evacuated, there were few lights shining around.

She had just listened to the 10 p.m. tropical update on the Weather Channel and wouldn't stay up for the next one in an hour. Stella was still creeping northward; the term moseying came to mind. It appeared Stella would not have enough time to strengthen before making landfall on the path she had set.

Stella has finally decided to arrive at the dance.

Looking up again, Rose realized the backyard was now pitch black. Patrick must have shut off the workshop's lights and would be heading in soon. She waited to see his form come around the back of the house and into the glow of the back-porch light. Soon they would head to bed. Gertie Mae and Butch were already snuggled side by side in their sheepskin sleeping caves, and their old girl Ruby was rolled into a tight ball on their bed. The dogs had called it a night hours ago when the time spans between rain bands became almost nil.

Patrick entered and shook off the long drover's coat he favored in rain storms. Hanging it on the hook by the door, he saw Rose standing by her map at the kitchen counter.

"What's the forecast chief?" Patrick moved to the sink to wash his hands. The scent of Hoppes #9 powder and Tung oil followed him through the kitchen.

"Sometime after midnight near Houma as a Two." Rose put the mug from her nightly cup of hot tea next to the sink.

Patrick dried his hands with a red checked dishcloth and looked at a photo of their camp affixed to the side of the frig. Patrick's hunting camp sat about three hours north of Baton Rouge.

Rose suspected he was thinking about who the camp would fare when Stella blew by. *It would be safe as long as a tornado didn't hit it.*

Hanging the dish towel on a drawer handle, Patrick started unbuttoning his shirt as he walked toward the bedroom.

"Let's enjoy the air conditioning while we've got it." Rose shared Patrick's dislike for sleeping in a warm room.

They had been through many storms over the years. The couple did their best to mentally block out the sounds of the wind whipping through the trees outside the bedroom windows as they settled in for the night. *It is what it is*, Rose thought of her mother's favorite saying.

Rest tonight, Rose thought as she drifted off to sleep to the sound of Patrick's soft snoring. Experience told her there would be one heck of a mess to clean up in the morning.

*

Katie lay on the guest room bed, trying to relax enough to fall asleep. The sheer curtains on the large window moved as the humid breeze flew in. She had cracked the window enough to allow for some air to enter, but not enough to let in the rain that had been falling off, but mainly on, for hours.

The air entering the room was musty and verdant. Katie had always thought that rain smelled clean. Somehow tonight's rain was different. Breathing deeply, she caught the scent of pine and a whiff of rosemary from the bush Lola had outside the window. Lola had claimed she needed a guaranteed supply of the fresh herb for her Thanksgiving turkey recipe.

After hearing stories of life in southern Louisiana without air conditioning, Katie was surprised that she felt rather comfortable at the moment. A cool sponge bath, light sleeping shorts with a matching t-shirt and her insulated cup of ice water next to the bed all helped. The damp breeze reminded her of being at Girl Scout camp during those hot, muggy Tennessee summers. Memories of trying to sleep with 15 other girls in the old log cabin bunk house made her smile. Katie had been able to sleep then, once the giggling and whispers quieted for the night.

Katie had been able to get a text through to her parents an hour ago letting them know she was well and safe. She mentioned their wild game feast in an effort to make her situation sound more like a hurricane party than a forced staycation.

Weathering the Storm

The quiet hours the trio shared looked nothing like the parties Katie had heard about on the news during previous storms. Lola and Rene had laughed when she mentioned them. Her hostess explained that rowdy parties were more for the young who had few responsibilities and little sense. Noting the glance Lola gave her husband and the slight grin on his ruddy face, Katie imagined there might have been a few such gatherings for the couple in the days before their kids were born and they had a home to protect.

The essence of pine tree also brought to mind the photos she had seen from Hurricane Katrina of houses damaged by trees toppled in the wind. Remembering Rene's tales involving the tall, willowy conifers imitating knives and butter, Katie mentally calculating the height of the pines in Lola's yard and their distance from the house. She laughed and decided she'd never sleep if she worried about the trees.

Rolling over, she looked for a cooler side to her pillow. Katie now faced the darkened window and was treated to a flash of lighting. As she counted 'one Mississippi, two Mississippi', Katie calculated how far away the lightening was. Unconsciously, she recited the prayer her mother said with her each night when she was a small child.

Now I lay me down to sleep. I pray the Lord my soul to keep. If I should………

When she finished, her eyes remained closed, blocking out the tumult outside the window. Katie envisioned the policemen on patrol and one officer in particular. Jake the cop who could also fix an air conditioner. Katie had to admit to herself that she found him rather impressive. What kind of man works all day outdoors in a hurricane without receiving a pay check? Not many that she knew. As a frequent volunteer through her church and the local ladies' civic club, Katie understood the good feeling of accomplishment she received when she helped others. But cooking in a soup kitchen or volunteering at the hospital did not involve anything dangerous.

Jake must be a unique individual to go that extra mile.

Although Katie remembered him back at the police station in uniform, it was the smiling AC repairman in the battered Tennessee hat she saw as she fell asleep to the constant patter of rain on the glass.

29.2N, 90.6W. 100 MPH. 90 miles southwest of Rienville. Hurricane Stella made landfall at 1:32 a.m. near the town of Cocodrie, Louisiana as a Category 2 storm. Residents of Southeast Louisiana should be aware the storm brings damaging winds and the possibility of tornados miles from the eye of the storm. Stella has started to dissipate and will continue to lose strength as it moves north toward Mississippi. NHC/NOAA.

Stella rolled inland like a woman with attitude. She made her entrance near Cocodrie, with her strongest winds moving out toward Grand Isle and beyond. Her winds blew through Bayou Oiseaux, moving the cypress trees like a metronome on crack. A waterspout formed over the frantic waves pouring inland. The mini tornado moved through the bay, picking up fish and marsh grass along the shoreline and depositing it all further down the bayou. Parts of camps and boat docks joined the other detritus swirling in the cloud. By the time it dissipated, the access road to James and Beryl's homes was two feet deep in soggy grass, mingled with misplaced crab traps and debris from different homes.

In town, Stella's winds made whirling dervishes of the tall pines. The live oaks, veterans of more hurricanes and tropical storms than any of the human residents of the town, moved more like dancers enjoying a waltz.

The rain at times exceeded the dreaded inch per hour max, overwhelming the drainage systems of many neighborhoods. Water filled the roadways and moved up driveways and into front yards. As the rain bands passed, the waters would recede for a time. Since the river closest to Rienville had already been near flood stage, the rainwater going into the catch basins at street level had no place to go. The slosh effect, hydrologists called it. Indeed, people would be sloshing through flooding caused by the storm for a day or two.

Acting like a gardener bent on pruning, Stella's sustained winds brought down dead branches from trees and uprooted palms with their shallow root balls. Twigs the size of baseball bats littered yards and many smaller pieces clogged street drains.

As trees came down, so did parts of the power grid. It would be a muggy night and the coming days would prove to be uncomfortable for many. Houses built to keep in the air conditioning were not conducive to allowing good air flow.

With the exception of the people working at the emergency operation's center, the hospital and a few insomniacs, Stella's arrival in Rienville was witnessed by the few awake as more of a whisper than a roar.

*

The crash penetrated Katie's pleasant dream. Jerking into a sitting position, for a moment she didn't recognize where she was. Katie had been dreaming she was at the beach, dozing off if her chair in the shallows, lulled by the waves coming in. But the crash had not been from waves on a sandy beach. It had come from outside the window. The room was inky black, and she could see a faint outline of the curtains moving in the darkness when lightening flashed. The wind was rattling the windows and rain continued to fall.

Since she was awake, Katie got out of bed and put on her flip flops. *Might as well use the time wisely.* She moved toward the bathroom. Keeping a hand along the wall, she walked slowly down the dark hall and noticed a glow coming from around the corner. Passing by her original destination, Katie found Lola sitting at the kitchen table. There was a book in front of her and a battery-operated lantern casted a glow over the pages.

"I wondered if you had heard that." Lola said as she noticed the young woman standing in the doorway. She placed the quilted bookmark on top of the page and closed the book.

Her young guest moved into the kitchen and sat down across from her.

Weathering the Storm

"I wondered if I had dreamed it," Katie said softly. She couldn't see anything through the kitchen window. It was amazing how truly dark it could be in the middle of town.

"No such luck. I believe we lost one of the younger pines in the front yard. Or maybe in the Smith's yard."

"Why don't you take out the pines? I've seen the pictures from Katrina. They seem to cause so much damage and they don't give you a lot of shade.

Lola sighed and peered through the window to see the outline of pines in the back yard.

"First, I hate the thought of killing a living tree for no reason. They help clean the air and more importantly, they drink an incredible amount of water. With our drainage issues, our backyard would be even more of a swamp than it normally is." Lola took a drink from her cup and looked over the rim at Katie. "Rene thinks I'm silly, but the main reason is I think they smell heavenly, especially when it rains like now. They remind me of home."

"You could plant new trees." Katie thought about lying in a hammock in the shade. "Maples would give you shade, and magnolias smell lovely when they bloom."

"True." Lola caressed the soft leather cover of her book. "But it would take years for them to grow. The dogs already make a big enough mess in the yard without adding more moisture to their playground. But really, we've talked to a friend who's an arborist. Pine trees growing in a cluster cut the wind for each other and are less apt to be toppled in a strong wind. It's the lone trees that are buffeted most at times like this. If I had to make a guess, I'd say the crash we heard was from a sickly lone tree that was in the doctor's office parking lot behind us. We'll have to see in the morning. I just hope it didn't take out our fence."

The friends sat in silence for a while, gazing out the window at nothingness.

"I'd think you'd sleep through this. You've been through so many storms." Katie admired Lola's calm demeanor. Thinking on it a bit, Katie decided Lola looked serene most of the time.

"No, even in this heat, the dogs want to snuggle. That just makes me feel like I'm in a steam oven. Plus, the pressure from the storm is hell on my ears." Lola ran her hands through the hair beside her face and pulled it back behind her ears.

"I hadn't noticed anything with my ears," Katie wondered out loud.

"I have some issues with my hearing. I've taken some medicine and I'm waiting for it to kick in. Then I'll try to sleep again. I do love to fall asleep to the sound of the rain."

They sat quietly for a moment.

"Has Stella made landfall yet?" It seemed to Katie that the rain and wind had been around for weeks instead of less than two days. Sitting in the kitchen now, she had noticed a difference in the weather. At times, the rain seemed to fall almost sideways and with an increased intensity.

"Yes, she did. About an hour ago, according to the app on my phone. She was barely a Two with winds right at one hundred miles per hour at the center." A loud gust drew Katie's attention back to the window. The back door was also moving slightly in its frame.

"What we have to be vigilant about now is tornados. We're under a watch until tomorrow night. While the storm is passing, it can spin them off with the bands of rain."

"I haven't heard a tornado siren since I've moved here." Katie had grown up with Wednesday noon tests of Nashville's early warning system.

"That's because we don't have them. Where I grew up, we had them too. I've always wondered why they don't have them on top of the fire houses here." Lola saw the look of concern on Katie's face.

"No worries." Lola held up her cell phone again. "From the wonderful world of cellphones comes a warning app that puts out an ungodly wail when a tornado is in the parish. Believe me, it can wake the dead. That's one of the reason's we make sure we keep the phones charged." Lola took a sip of her water and put her glass back on the table. "If you hear the alarm, head to the laundry room. It's our only room without windows."

Katie rose from her chair and tucked it in under the table. "Then I guess we just ride out the proverbial storm, right?" Katie asked her fellow restless sleeper.

"That's all we can do," Lola stood and put her cup in the kitchen sink. "Might as well try to get some sleep," Lola said as she walked toward the master bedroom door.

"Sounds good. Sleep well." Katie turned toward her original destination. She decided to leave her bedroom door cracked and prayed she would not hear Lola's tornado app go off in the night.

30.4N, 90.4W. 50 MPH. 80 miles west of Rienville.

"Will it ever stop raining?" Katie walked into the humid kitchen. Rene was removing an old camp-style percolating coffee pot from the gas range and poured himself a cup. She could smell the rich aroma of chicory mixed with the roasted beans.

Motioning with his mug, Rene wordlessly asked if she'd like to join him. Receiving a nod, he reached for one of the brightly colored mugs and filled it with the brew.

"Milk is in the cooler." Rene leaned against the counter and enjoyed a sip.

"I'm good." Katie put the mug to her nose and inhaled deeply before taking the first drink. "It's crazy that I'd want to drink something so hot when it's so warm in here."

"The heart wants what it wants." He smiled as he enjoyed his coffee and heard his wife coming down the hall.

"Morning sunshine," he said as Lola moved through the doorway. She did not respond as much as nod her head. Lola reached for a cup with a quilt pattern painted on the front amongst the mugs hanging under a cabinet. Lola knew what she looked like. Her husband would affectionately call her a hot mess. Lola was wearing an old Rush t-shirt over faded denim pants cut short for working in the yard. She had tried to pull her hair into what was supposed to be a pony tail but really resembled more of a rat's nest. Knowing she looked very tired from her nocturnal reading session, she was grateful Rene kept any comments about her appearance to himself. Lola held out her cup and her husband poured her first cup of the day.

With her eyes closed, she savored the first taste of dark roasted brew. A small smile bloomed from her lips and she helped herself to another sip before opening her eyes to look at the people in her kitchen. They both eyed her with funny expressions.

"What, you've never seen a woman drink a cup of coffee before?" Lola asked as she took another sip.

"I wish you'd look at me with as much love as you are that cup of coffee," Rene said with a grin. Katie produced an unladylike snort into her mug but said nothing.

Weathering the Storm

"You wish." Lola leaned into her husband's side and smiled. Rene laid his arm around her shoulder and took another drink of coffee. Katie was a bit envious at how content the couple looked together. Lola turned to their young friend. "Did you get any sleep? It got a bit louder outside after we closed down our chat."

"I did. I guess I finally worked myself to sleep. The rain does have a lulling effect once you get past the sounds of things crashing to the ground."

"There is that," Rene commented as he walked to the front door. He gave a low whistle as he walked out onto the porch. Their dog Blue followed him out the doorway, sniffing the air before moving down the steps. He went looking for a dry place to do his business. It would be hard as there was standing water just about everywhere.

"Well Lola, looks like we're an island for a while," he said, sipping his coffee. The two women had followed him out the door and saw the water within a few feet of reaching the rear tires on Katie's car.

"I'm glad you told me to pull all the way up to the house," she said, looking at the other houses in the cul-du-sac. The few cars still in evidence were also sitting high.

"No problem," Rene said, as he called Blue back from the water. He was exploring and the water was up to the dog's belly.

"I'd think he'd be happy being a water dog." Katie sensed the canine was pouting about having to go inside. He was moving very slowly back toward the house.

"I know he loves to run around. I worry he'll run into a mat of ants. It would not be pretty," Rene said, petting Blue on the head as he came to sit by his side. Katie had heard about the floating masses of fire ants during flooding like this. One of her neighbors had warned her about them when Katie experienced her first real deluge.

"The water will go down as the day wears on. We'll just have to wait it out." Lola looked at the waist deep lake that was their street.

As they walked back into the house and Lola went to get a beach towel to clean up the dog, Katie realized the area around Lola's house was quiet. The Normandy's generator was temporarily off. No hum from the refrigerator or the window unit down the hall. She asked Lola about the silence.

"Yeah, sometime in the night the generator ran out of gas. I don't know when it did, but it was warm when we woke up. The frig should be fine until we refill it with gas."

Katie moved into the kitchen while Rene moved past and entered the garage. After getting toweled dry, Blue assumed his favorite position on the canvas dog bed. He closed his eyes, exuding contentment.

"What can I do to help?" Katie asked as Lola hung the towel across the back of a kitchen chair by the back door.

"There's really nothing at the moment. If you're hungry for breakfast, I've got bagels you can toast in a pan on the stove and you can finish up the cream cheese in the cooler. There's also cereal in the pantry and half a quart of milk left. Fruit's on the counter. Help yourself to anything you see."

Katie decided the unique bagel toasting method would make a good story for her parents, so she made one for herself and another for Lola. Her friend told her to not worry about Rene as he wasn't a breakfast person.

30.9N, 90.2W. 90 MPH. 80 miles northwest of Rienville.

Patrick came into the kitchen after checking out his gunsmithing workshop. Entering the mud room, he slipped off the white rubber boots and put on his canvas slippers. The house was abnormally quiet since the power went out sometime in the night.

Rose sat in front of the large picture window in the kitchen, looking comfortable in her cotton nightgown. She had already told her husband that her plan was to stay in her jammies the entire day just because she could. Rose would not have to worry about clients calling today, she hoped. The latest edition from a series by her favorite mystery author was opened in front of her and her ever present diet soda sitting by her book.

"How's it looking out there?" Rose asked her husband and resident caretaker. She thanked God daily for Patrick's presence in her life for many reasons; home handyman often being at the top of the list.

"No major damage. Only a few large branches were on the roof, but nothing went through the shingles." He had wadded around the house in his shrimp boots and made a similar assessment of the house. Where their property was concerned, Stella had strolled through, leaving little reminders in her wake.

"There's just a lot of debris to clean up before I have to mow again." As they looked at the amount of water standing in the yard, Rose reasoned that would not be anytime soon.

"Good to hear." Her head lowered as she returned to her story. Without looking at the bottle, she reached over and picked up the soda for a swig.

The sound of a vehicle coming down their gravel drive took them a bit by surprise. They had thought visitors would have a hard time getting around in the aftermath of Stella's landing. Moving to the front of the house, Rose looked out the window while Patrick went to the door. After checking through the side window, he opened the door to see a high-water vehicle bearing an official police decal on the side coming to a stop behind his old truck. Patrick walked out to see his friend Keith Ogeron and another officer he did not know get down from the cab.

"What brings you out this way Keith," Patrick asked as he received a handshake from the officer.

"Just checking on our favorite gunsmith. Patrick, this is Jake Mesch, one of new reserve officers." Ogeron motioned toward the other officer.

Patrick gave the young man a hearty handshake and wished him good luck with the department. Patrick had an arrangement with the police department that he would do any repairs on the officer's private guns or the department's service weapons for free. It was his way to contribute. Patrick knew the officers, who earned way too little in his often-expressed opinion, appreciated the service.

"We did fine. Just some clean up once the water goes down. How did the city fare? We haven't been able to get much news."

"Overall, better than expected. There are downed trees and a few power lines. All in all, it was a moderate storm," Ogeron said. "The only severe damage seems to be from a tornado that spun over Bayou Oiseaux. We've gotten word there are some camps there that are in pretty bad shape." The officer noted the concern on his friend's face and added, "from what we've learned, only a few places got hit, not all of them."

After a few more minutes of town news, the officers climbed back into the tall truck, laboriously turned the oversized truck around and drove down the driveway. Patrick watched them leave and then went back into the house.

"That was quite a conversation," Rose said. "What's the scoop on town?"

"Rienville did fair. Nothing major. Keith was telling me there are reports of twister damage in Bayou Oiseaux. Isn't that where Lola's Dad lives?"

"Yes, James' camp is out there. I wonder if Lola had heard from him." She moved into the kitchen and tried calling her friend on her cellphone. The automated message noting an overloaded system greeted her. She tried texting but it would not send. "I can't get through to Lola."

Patrick went back to the front window and looked at the water covering the street. He could tell it was receding slowly by where the

Weathering the Storm

edge of the water was compared to the high-water mark made of leaves and pine needles further up the lawn.

"Let's sit tight for another hour and see how far the water goes down. You can keep trying to reach her. If we don't get any more rain, we could probably make it into Lola's house or at least close enough to wade the last few blocks.

"I knew I wasn't going to be able to stay in my jammies all day." Rose mumbled as she walked toward the increasingly warm master bedroom and the rest of her day.

31.1N, 89.4W. 30 MPH. 60 miles north of Rienville. Final Advisory for interests along the Gulf Coast. Hurricane Stella has been downgraded to a Tropical Depression as it moves through Mississippi. NHC/NOAA.

Lola and Katie were picking up fallen branches from the hickory trees in the front yard when the ancient blue Ford truck turned at the corner and headed toward them. As the truck crept up the street, it made a small wake through the water still standing in the street. Lola gathered her scraps and pressed them down in the black trash bag her friend held open.

The truck's engine went silent in the driveway. Patrick bounced out of the truck and gave Lola a smile. "Your old man lying around the house?"

"He's in the backyard checking the drains. We've still got a mess of water standing by the back fence." Lola watched as Patrick, looking comfortable in his jeans and shrimp boots despite the heat, gave her a wave and headed for the fence's side gate.

By the time he went through, Rose had exited the truck and walked over to her friends. Dressed in denim capris and a faded Cubs t-shirt and boots to match her husband's, she looked ready for working outside.

"What's the news from your Dad?" Rose crouched down to pick up a handful of the small branches from the pile. A leaf floated down around her head to land nearby.

"No word so I am thinking no news is good news."

Rose looked up to see Katie watching her. The young ones can be more perceptive at times, Rose thought.

"We got a visit from a couple of Rienville's finest this morning. They were doing wellness checks in the area. They said the Bayou Oiseaux area sustained some damage from either a small tornado or a waterspout. I'm sure your Daddy's fine, but we wanted to let you know the latest."

Lola stopped cleaning up branches and tied the large garbage bag. Katie took it from her hands and walked it down to the curb to add to the pile slowly growing. She wiped the sweat dripping down her forehead with the sleeve of her t-shirt, leaving a smudge above her eye.

Weathering the Storm

Walking back toward the two women, Katie could see the tension in Lola's shoulders as she and Rose talked quietly.

"Rene and I had planned on going out there tomorrow, thinking the water would be off most of the roads by then. I need to talk to Rene, but I think we probably need to head over there sooner rather than later." She had tied a red bandana as a head scarf to keep her hair out of her eyes and off her neck. Pulling the fabric off, she unrolled it, turned it inside out to a cleaner side and wiped her face and neck before twisting it again and tying up her silver hair again.

As her friends agreed that a trip to the bayou was necessary, they walked up to the front porch and toward the pitcher of iced tea that beaconed from its place on the railing.

*

"Hey." Patrick called to his friend, muck gripping his rubber boots as he traipsed across the yard. There was standing water rippling through tall grass that needed to be cut. It would grow considerably higher before a mower could make it through without bogging down.

"Hey. You guys fair ok?" Rene was propping up a portion of fence that had taken a hit from a heavy limb and was leaning too far off vertical. Once the ground was dry, Rene would install a new post and secure it, good as new since no boards had broken.

"We did fine. Power's out, but that's to be expected." Patrick put his shoulder against the planks and shoved while Rene wedged the support beam deeper into the ground.

Rene took out his handkerchief and wiped the moisture from his glasses before replacing them on the bridge of his nose. The two men surveyed the yard, accessing what needed to be done next.

"Keith Ogeron and a new deputy named Mesch stopped by the house. They said there's damage on Bayou Oiseaux. More than just water, maybe a small tornado or waterspout. Did James stay out there?"

The men had walked over to a large limb lying in the corner of the yard. More than six feet long and as thick as his arm, Rene was happy for the help in moving it onto some saw horses. He'd have to use his chain saw to take off the branches and cut it into pieces before he could take it to the street. It would be picked up by people looking to restock their fire wood stash for the winter.

"Lola hasn't heard anything for the past few days. Losing power before the storm hit was not helpful. I know she's worried." The men rested the log on the cutting stand with a grunt. "The ol' goat is a tough one. He'll get us word when he can. With what you've just said though, we need to get to his camp sooner rather than later just in case he does need help."

"He is that. Let me know if you need help at his place," Patrick brushed the pine bark off his hands as the men turned toward the house and the promise of a cold drink.

*

Lola had initially been content to stay at home and wait for word from her father. Stella had arrived in the night. She knew it was unrealistic for him to call her since some of the cell towers had been damaged and now the electricity was off in most of the parish. Lola had tried to keep herself busy picking up the yard and other mindless work while visiting with Katie.

After Rose and Patrick left, the women had finished clearing the front yard of debris. Lola then returned to cleaning the house. Her impression of the Energizer bunny was starting to concern Rene.

Stopping Lola on a pass through the kitchen, Rene gathered her in a loose hug.

"Let's take a ride to your Dad's place." Despite the heat, she wrapped her arms around his waist and gave him a sweaty hug.

"Do you think we can get to him?"

"Won't know until we try. I'll get the truck keys."

Weathering the Storm

Lola knew it was highly improbable they could reach her dad's camp because of the debris from the storm surge. Previous experience had taught her that. But trying was better than doing nothing. Plus, the roadway wasn't the only route available to get to her Dad.

They had quietly loaded their kayaks into the back of Rene's truck and tied them down along with the life preservers and paddles. Trying not to draw attention to what he was doing, Rene placed his upgraded first aid kit into a dry sack and tied it to his kayak. Along with your standard Band-Aids and antiseptic wipes, it contained items you'd need to treat anything from snake bites to broken bones to gunshot wounds. Bayous are beautiful and challenging places. Careful respect for what could happen within its boundaries was always prudent.

Driving out of their subdivision, they saw people slowly cleaning up the debris and moving downed trees off the road ways. The drone of chain saws reverberated through the air as they passed the city limits. After being stuck inside for the past few days, people needed to get out and move about, taking control of their lives again.

As the couple neared the backroads leading to her father's camp, they passed the boardwalk. It seemed like more than just a few days ago, Lola had talked to the young couple as they made ready for their outdoor wedding. The wooden walkway was overwhelmed by marsh grass and the parking lot was littered with broken branches and Spanish moss. The remnants of a once beautiful white satin bow waved from a tall pole at the base of the boardwalk. Lola saw the flowing material as a memento from one significant event that had taken place there in the last few days. The debris field surrounding the ribbon was testament to the other.

Lola said a silent prayer for the young couple and their families. *Such a tremulous start to a marriage could set the course for the rest of their lives.* Either they learned that together they could handle anything, or they could treat it as an omen of trials to come. She prayed it would be the first.

Earthy smells grew stronger as the mounds of washed up marsh grass sat piled along the tree line and reached over the road way. Bodies of dead nutria and egrets lay mixed amid the grasses, bloating in the heat. The scent of decay was evident and would become overwhelming in the coming days as bacteria had a heyday.

Turning right onto his father-in-law's access road, Rene was thankful for their four-wheel drive and his high wheel bed. Since the trees grew tall along each side of the oyster shell road, it was easy to see the way even though the shells had disappeared under the displaced detritus from the marsh.

Soon after leaving the highway and passing a sharp turn, Rene hit the brakes and came to a stop. A large water oak, more than a hundred years old or more, lay partially across the road and blocking their way. Rene swore under his breath, put the truck in park and opened his door. Standing on the running board, he viewed the obstacle in their path.

"If we had a four-wheeler, we could probably get around it and still avoid the ditch. The truck can't make it Lola. It's too wide."

Lola looked out the windshield at the road ahead. What was usually a lovely drive down to the bayou was a mess.

"I know we could walk, but I don't think that's wise," he said, still staring straight ahead. Lola knew Patrick hated giving her bad news. The blocked road was not what she wanted to see.

Lola let out a deep breath. "I know you're right. There are probably water moccasins in that mess just waiting for someone to come by." Looking out the passenger window, she blinked back tears of frustration. Once again, she thought about how much easier the past few days would have been if her stubborn father had come to stay at her house.

"On to Plan B." Lola turned to Rene and tried to smile a bit. It was not his fault her father could be referred to as a hind end of a mule.

Nodding, Rene moved the gear shift to reverse. He put his arm across the back of the bench seat and gave Lola's shoulder a squeeze in the process. Rene looked out the back window and slowly backed down the road. It would take a while as he was unwilling to try to turn the truck around in the muck.

After what seemed like a very long and slow process, Rene brought the truck back onto the highway and drove toward the closest boat launch. As the crow flies, it was less than a mile from his father-in-law's place. Paddling in by water, it was at least twice as far away.

Although the condition of the boat launch was similar to the rest of the area, it showed signs that someone had made an attempt to clean it up a bit. A path had been made to the concrete driveway into the water and two cars with empty boat trailers sat to one side of the parking lot.

Rene parked as close to the launch as was practical due to the mess and shut off the engine. He and Lola got out and untied the kayaks. As the boats became free, the couple carried them to the water's edge. After everything was out of the truck bed, Rene moved the truck. There was still space under the wide limbs of an ancient live oak amongst the other vehicles waiting for their owners to return.

The unloading was done in relative silence. The couple had been making kayak trips for so many years, general communication wasn't necessary. They saved their words for pointing out interesting sights along the bank or boaters going past. After donning their life vests and pushing off, they started paddling toward the camp. As expected, the water was filled with debris. They floated past large tree branches, floating mounds of marsh grass and more dead animal carcasses. There were also pieces of buildings bobbing on the surface and along the banks. Not too much, but enough for Lola to be concerned. Again, she reminded herself that her father was a tough old bird who was indestructible. At least he thought so, Lola grimaced.

Coming from this direction, they passed Ms. Beryl's house first. Sadness came over Lola as she saw grass and sticks covering the women's impeccably groomed camellia garden. Ms. Beryl was known across the parish for her camellias and most of her prized bushes lay crushed under the debris.

Holding their paddles still, the two floated quietly as they surveyed the yard.

"She'll be so sad when she sees this." Lola maneuvered closer to the bank.

"I'm afraid the salt water that came in did as much damage as the muck." Rene paddled backwards so he could see the far side of the house.

"Shit," he swore and dug his paddle hard through the water to get closer to the bank for a better look. Lola didn't like the sound of that and followed Rene to where he had stopped. Looking at the back corner of the house, Lola could see that a corner of the building had been knocked off by the skinny pine lying on the ground surrounded by bricks and shingles.

"Well it could be worse. She'll have some water damage. It may be relegated to that one room. I think that's her kitchen."

"I think she'll be more upset about her garden." Lola worked to keep her boat from drifting in the mild current.

"I believe you're right. She seems to be more worried about living things than just plain stuff. I have always liked that about her." Rene turned his boat around. "I think it's safe to say she's not here." He maneuvered the front of the kayak downstream.

"No, if she was, she'd be working on the damage, Dad alongside her. They must be at Dad's place." Lola had noticed Ms. Beryl's car was not sitting in the driveway.

Despite the destruction surrounding them, Lola thought the bayou still looked beautiful. Just off the bow of her boat, the sunlight turned the café au lait water into a dusty green. Diamonds sparkled on the top of the water. After all the rain, the air was clean and smelled of the cedar and the bald cypress that grew in the wetlands at the water's edge.

The debris in the water thickened as they got closer to James' camp. At one point, the pair met a bottleneck of tree parts, broken lumber and lost crab traps. Rene paddled from one bank to another, looking for a path that led through the obstacle. More importantly to Lola, she could not see her Dad's place since it lay around the next bend.

Rene sat back in his seat and rested the paddle across his lap. He opened the bottle of water he had sitting in the cup holder and took a long swig. Reaching across the water, he shared the tepid drink with Lola. Taking out his handkerchief and taking off his hat, he wiped the sweat from his forehead and neck.

"For now, I believe the road ends here." To sooth this conscience, Rene continued to look for another option around the obstacle.

"Do you think we could walk the rest of the way?" Lola looked stressed but hopeful as she paddled to sit by the shoreline.

"Normally I'd say yes. But there's going to be some unhappy critters in all the marsh grass and underbrush we'd have to traipse through. It's just not safe. We also didn't bring snake boots or our waders. We need to head home Lola and look for another way in."

The couple sat quietly as the water flowed passed them and they looked down the bayou toward the camp they could not reach.

"Think he's alright?" Lola voiced her fear. She knew if Rene thought her Dad was in any real danger, he'd have found a way through all of the obstacles hours before.

"He's an old son of a gun who's been through worse. He and Spot and Ms. Beryl are probably sitting on the porch and fishing off the railing," Rene said with a smile. He almost believed it himself. Although he resented James for putting Lola through this scenario again, Rene had to admire the man that at his age did not let a little storm rule his world.

"We'll head back and see what our options are." Rene guided his boat back the way they came. Lola took a last swig of water and put the bottle in her cup holder. With a last look down the bayou, she turned her kayak and followed Rene toward home.

*

Katie brushed out her hair and pulled it into a pony tail. High on the back of her head, it allowed a little air to get to the back of her neck. As she sat in the reading chair in the corner of the guest room, Katie pulled out her blessings book from her duffle bag. The small notebook had a colorful cover and an elastic band that kept the book closed when not in use. Pulling one of her favorite gel pens from the binding, she opened the cover and flipped the pages to the next blank space.

Her mother's mother had given Katie her first blessings book when she was a teenager. Katie had stayed with her grandma for part of each summer during those years. Although she had had a quiet life compared to many of her friends, there was the usual angst that came with growing up; cycling hormones and teenage drama in general. Grandma had strongly suggested she write down one or two things she was thankful for at the end of each day before going to bed. Katie performed what she saw as a silly chore that first summer. She recognized her grandmother had given her the gift out of love and she adored the older woman. Surprisingly, Katie continued her nightly writings for years to come. When she had packed her bags for college, she left the volumes on her bedroom shelf as a sign that she didn't need such a childish thing as a blessings journal when she was all grown up.

It didn't take long for Katie to realize she missed the contentment she received when she wrote down the positive things that had happened each day. It was a short time later Katie had picked up a small journal at the campus bookstore and started the practice again.

On this humid night, Katie paged through the past several days and reviewed her entries. There was Dr. MacDermitt's name and she had noted the quiet mammogram technician. Having health insurance was on the page as well.

Uncapping the pen, she chose simpler things today. 'Air conditioning,' which she didn't have. 'Ice water,' a true blessing in itself. Slowly, she continued to write, 'Lola', 'Rene' and 'the smell of rosemary coming through the window'.

Weathering the Storm

*

After loading up, Lola and Rene drove toward Rose's house. Dodging the trash on the road, they made good time. After they arrived, Lola updated Rose as to what they had found. Rene made his way to the Patrick's workshop in the backyard.

"So, the damage does not sound too bad," Patrick said, brushing the sawdust off his apron. He'd been working on a new rifle stock when Rene had knocked on the door.

"I've seen worse. I have to agree it looks more like a tornado went through than just the expected wind damage from a hurricane. Trouble is all the trees and stuff in the water. If James is back there and didn't take a direct hit from a twister, I'm sure he's fine. Lola knows that, but she needs to lay eyes on him to rest her mind." Rene picked up a can of Tung oil. He had always liked visiting Patrick's workshop. It reminded him of an old toymaker's workshop he had visited when he was a child. Odd looking tools and metal cans with strange names.

Taking off his apron, Patrick hung it on a wall peg. He started to turn off the battery-operated lights he was using to illuminate his workbench since electricity had not been restored.

"Since you can't reach him and he was last known to be in a disaster area, and because of his age…", Patrick said as he moved through the building.

"Don't let James hear you call him old," Rene laughed.

"Never. But he's unaccounted for so I think you should notify the sheriff's office."

"Agreed. We can head over there now." Rene had lost his smile as he moved toward the door.

"I'll go with you. Can't do much more here until the power comes on."

As they walked toward the house, the men could hear their wives talking through the open kitchen windows. No doubt it would be four people heading into the old part of the city, looking for the cavalry.

*

"Hello folks. What can we do for you?" The young woman gave them a bright smile. Wearing a sheriff's office t-shirt and her badge on her utility belt, Lola thought the young deputy looked way too young to protect and serve. *The guardians of the peace are getting younger by the day or I'm just feeling older by the minute.*

"We haven't been able to make contact with my Dad for several days. His name is James Coubillion and he lives on Bayou Oiseaux. We tried to reach him by truck and with our kayaks earlier today and it's a mess out there. We're looking for some help in trying to reach his home to check on him." Lola felt panic rise along with her voice as she made her request and did her best to dampen it down. Rene gently rubbed his hand up and down the small of her back as she spoke. He must have heard it too, she thought.

With a calm air Lola appreciated, the deputy gave her a clipboard bearing a form and a pen.

"If you would please, give us his name, his home address and his phone number. It also asks for a brief description. Add anything you think may help. Once you're done, we'll check to see who has information about that area." She motioned the group to several tables to her right as an older man walked in the door and moved toward her station.

As they sat quietly, Lola wrote the requested information on the form. She arose and returned to the deputy's desk.

"That should be everything." Lola passed the clipboard and pen to the woman who then looked it over.

"If you'll wait just a bit, I'll go back and see who you need to speak with. There are refreshments over in the corner. Please help yourselves. People have been so kind about bringing stuff in." She directed Lola toward the cookie trays. She waved at another deputy to take her place as she left the room.

"Anyone for coffee?" Lola walked across the floor. The group stood up and helped themselves to a snack and hot drinks. The coffee was surprising good, and someone had taken the time to bake cookies. They tasted like home. Taking the treats back to the table, the group ate and sipped in silence. Not five minutes later, Officer Mesch came through the doorway. After the requisite greetings and handshakes, Jake walked them back to a meeting room. A sheriff's deputy and an officer in a wildlife and fisheries uniform waited for them next to a table with a large map of the parish spread across the top. With a nod to Patrick, the member of the sheriff's department put out his hand to Lola and introduced himself as Deputy Brown and the other man as Officer Roebuck. After the introductions were finished, they all sat down. His work done, Jake quietly closed the door as he left the room.

"When did you last hear from Mr. Coubillion, Ms. Normandy?" Brown asked as he looked toward Lola, a pen hovered over his notepad.

"Three days ago. I have tried his cellphone and haven't been able to get through. First it was mostly due to lack of a signal. Now it's either turned off or the battery is dead."

"Where was he when you talked to him?"

"He was still in his house on Bayou Oiseaux. We were trying to talk him into coming to our house for the storm, but he's stubborn and said he wasn't ready to leave his house. He wanted to wait a bit longer to see what Stella would do." Lola frowned at Rene as she recited the last part.

"We tried to get to his house earlier today. The road is blocked by a large tree lying across the road. Then we tried to go in by water." After pointing out the location of the boat launch on the map, Rene let them know they couldn't go any further because of the large amount of debris blocking their way down the bayou. Deputy Brown transcribed the information to the paper.

"Dad was also concerned about his neighbor, Ms. Beryl. Beryl Brown." Looking at the wildlife officer, Lola asked if she was any relation.

"Not that I know of ma'am."

"Anyway, Dad was worried about Ms. Beryl because her house isn't raised, and they talked about weathering the storm at his house together."

"We were able to get to Ms. Beryl's place by kayak. It's got some significant tree damage, and no one appeared to be home. Her car was not in the driveway." Rene relayed the fact that all of their observations were from the water.

Officer Brown asked them to point out on the map the locations for both properties. Officer Roebuck looked over sheets of notes on the table before speaking.

"Earlier today I flew over this area in a helicopter. There's definitely damage to many of the camps, but nothing truly devastating. I did not see anyone in the general area you indicated. Usually in this type of situation, people will come out and wave at helicopters."

"There is a chance they didn't stay at home. However, I know they would have contacted me if they had left." Lola's concern carried through her tone. Rose, who had been sitting quietly at her side and observing the dialog, moved closer to Lola and put her arm around her friend's shoulder. Rene was already holding one of Lola's hands as they sat at the table.

The officers talked amongst themselves for a few minutes, gesturing at the map and other papers on the desk. Brown turned to Lola.

"Mrs. Normandy, normally we have to wait twenty-four hours from the time a report is made on a missing person before we can authorize an active search. The storm and your father's last location allows for some leeway in the timing. Wildlife and Fisheries has loaned us the use of an airboat for the duration of this storm response. We can put in at a boat landing near Mr. Coubillion's place and see if we can get to his house. It can go places normal boats can't. There are still a few hours of daylight left. Can you and your husband accompany us if we go now?"

Weathering the Storm

"Of course," Lola quickly stood up with Rene following her lead. "We can leave from here." She turned to Rose and before she could say anything else, Rose put up a hand. "Don't worry about us. We'll get a ride home." Rose hugged her friend and stayed with Patrick as they watched the anxious couple leave with the parish's version of the cavalry.

"Let's find that ride." Patrick said as they moved into the hallway. Seeing Officer Mesch as they passed the kitchen, Patrick called out to the man and secured a ride courtesy of the Rienville Police Department.

*

Sitting in the back of a police car was a new experience for Rose. Patrick rode up front with Officer Mesch. After getting her husband to take a picture of her smiling through the protective screen between the seats to send to her friends later, she started to call Katie to give her an update.

When she was just about to press the call button, the young man laughed at something Patrick said. Rose liked the sound of the young man's laugh. *Joyful.* Remembering her visit with Katie to the sandbag station and upon further reflection on the handsome young man driving, Rose decided not to call after all and put the phone face down in her lap.

In a few minutes, they arrived home. Since the backdoors lacked handles, Officer Mesch got out of the car and helped her out of the back seat.

"Thanks for the ride Jake," Patrick called to him as he rounded the car. Evidently, her husband and the young man were now on a first name basis. Talk of deer hunting in the fall will do that to a couple of guys.

161

"Yes, thank you Jake. It would have been a long walk." She smiled as he closed the door and turned to get back into the unit. "I was wondering if you could do me a favor on your way back to the station."

"I will if I can. How can I help you?" Jake's expression was open as he rested an arm over the top of the driver's side door. She knew he had probably been on duty for much of the past few days and was genuinely worn down. Rose appreciated Jake was still willing to be helpful.

"You remember my friend Katie from the day we met filling sand bags? She's staying at the Normandy's house. I need to let her know about Lola and Patrick and the airboat trip. The cell service is so sporadic right now and their home phone is out. Would you mind stopping by there on your way back and let her know what's happening? We would really appreciate it." Rose gave Jake her best concerned mother smile.

"No problem. What's their address?" After writing it down, he confirmed it was indeed on his way and no inconvenience.

Standing in the driveway as the police car drove away, Patrick looked at his wife. He threw his arm over her shoulder before he raised his phone to Rose's face. His mobile showed four bars of signal strength.

"Phone troubles?"

As Rose slipped her own phone into her back pocket, she wrapped her other hand around the man's waist and turned him toward the house.

"Did I not mention taking Katie to fill a few sandbags? We met a very nice young man there….". She continued the story as they entered their hot and humid house and were greeted by their four-legged welcoming committee.

*

Katie had spent much of the afternoon in a rocking chair on the front porch. Despite the humidity, the porch was cooler than the house. Katie was still sitting there she saw the police cruiser pull into the

Weathering the Storm

driveway. Feeling a little uneasy, she relaxed a bit when she saw Jake Mesch get out of the car and walk up the driveway.

He was still dressed in the storm dictated casual uniform. When he got out of the car, he sat the dark blue baseball cap over his short, light brown hair.

"Hey," Katie called from the porch, as she started to rise from the chair.

"No need to get up." Jake was on the porch in a few strides. She settled back into the chair and returned to rocking at a steady rhythm. "Rose and Patrick sent me over with the latest news on the search for Mr. Coubillion."

Despite being anxious for the information, the manners Katie's mother had distilled in her automatically kicked in. Seeing the damp spots on his t-shirt told her refreshments would likely be a welcomed kindness.

"Before you tell me what's happening, can I get you a lemonade or some water? Both are ice cold."

"Lemonade sounds good, if it's no trouble."

"I was about to go in for a refill myself when you drove up. Have a seat and I'll be right back." She maneuvered around the man and headed to the door. Jake sat down in a matching rocking chair, pulling out a handkerchief from his back pocket to wipe the moisture from his neck.

As she filled two large to-go cups with ice, Katie checked her cell phone. Rose had not tried to call. *Hmmm, interesting.* Katie quickly texted, 'there's a police officer on the porch here' and sent the message on its way to Rose. As she poured the lemonade, the device pinged.

"Hope he's cute," she read out loud. "I forgot to ask about his Mawmaw. Please ask him for me." The text ended with a smiley face.

Really. Rose the matchmaker. Sighing, she pocketed her phone and carried the cups to the porch.

"Here you go." She handed Jake one cup and moved to the other chair. By the time Katie turned and sat down, his glass was half empty and he was smiling at her.

"That hit the spot. Thank you very much." He slowly moved the chair back and forth and the two people enjoyed what breeze there was at the moment.

"You said you had news?"

"Not really news so much as an update. Lola and Rene are going out on a Wildlife and Fisheries airboat to try to get to her Dad's house. Airboats can get to places regular boats can't right now. They didn't plan on coming back here before heading to the boat launch and Rose didn't want you to worry." As he took sip, Jake savored the drink's tartness along with the sweetness of present company.

"She's been so worried about him. I hope he's OK. I've only met him a few times. Mr. James is a character and I can just see him facing a storm on the deck of his camp." Katie smiled at the vision.

They talked a bit about Katie surviving her first storm and some of the calls he'd worked over the past few days. By the time a half hour had passed, the lemonade was gone, and he needed to get back to work. Luckily, no calls had come through on his radio. Katie had enjoyed talking with the man from the Volunteer State.

Jake got up to leave. He put his empty cup on the floor next to the chair. Katie rose as well and offered him a refill for the road. He declined.

As he stood on the porch, he took off his hat and held it loosely at his side. Katie's eyes followed the motion and then moved back to his face. "I was wondering, once they close the EOC, if you might like to get together for dinner or something?" Katie could tell Jake had made the request as casual as possible. After sharing this time on the porch, it only took a moment for her to realize how much she'd like to get to know him better.

Katie was already thinking to invite Jake to get together for coffee or something, even if he thought her action a bit forward. She had been sitting on the fence. The uncertainty of her test results dampened her enthusiasm. Now she had to make a decision. With this request,

Weathering the Storm

Katie remembered her mother telling her, 'Don't put up your umbrella until it starts to rain'.

"I'd like that." The grin on his face told Katie she had provided the correct answer. "How long will you be working at the center?"

"It shouldn't be more than a few more days at the most, according to what the regulars have told me. I've had people calling me about their air conditioning units, but I won't go back to my AC job until the center closes."

She took out her phone and looked up Jake's name in her contacts. Katie had entered his information in case she needed her air conditioner fixed and couldn't reach her landlord. At least that's what she had told herself. She selected her information and sent it to Jake's number. She heard a chirp come from his phone clipped on his utility belt.

"When your schedule is free, give me a call."

After putting on his hat, Jake pulled his phone from the holder and saw Katie's phone number on the screen. He returned the phone to its holder.

"I'll do that." He stepped off the porch and adjusted his hat. "Let me know if you have any problems with your house when you get back. I'd be happy to help."

"I'll do that. Stay safe out there."

Sending her a smile and a smart salute from behind his open car door, Katie watched him drive out of the cul-du-sac.

Realizing how much she looked forward to receiving that dinner call, Katie made a mental note to deliver a batch of her sugar cookies especially decorated with the Cubs' logo to Rose as soon as she moved back home. On the flip side, Katie decided to let Rose the matchmaker stew in her own juices for a while before she called with an update on Jake's Mawmaw.

She sat back into the rocking chair and enjoyed the quiet and the breeze.

*

Lola could not believe how loud the airboat's engine was. Even with protective earphones, the noise was almost deafening, and it sent vibrations through her entire body.

Rene and Lola were strapped into the lower front seats on the olive drab green boat, while Brown and Roebuck sat in taller seats behind them. Roebuck was driving the airboat through open water on the bay, heading toward the entrance to Bayou Oiseaux. As they entered the narrow waterway, the group started to encounter downed trees and pieces of homes that had until recently stood on the bayou's banks.

Roebuck slowed down considerably once they reached the mouth of the bayou. As they pushed toward James' camp, much of the flotsam was pushed aside by the curved front of the boat. He had warned everyone to be on the lookout for anything in their path that looked like it was planted firmly into the bottom and not floating. Hitting a stuck tree would provide a rude awakening for both the boat's hull and its passengers.

Rene and Lola recognized most of the camps they passed, as they had floated by them often over the years. Some were missing shingles and others had parts of decks gone. Most had mounds of the ever-present grass lying up against the pilings that held the buildings upright.

After moving down the bank about a half mile, Rene used a hand signal to point out their destination. Moving closer to the building, they could see a few broken windows as well as part of the deck had been torn off. James' boat sat askew in its straps, still securely tucked up under the house. His crab traps had not fared as well. Only a few were left on the side of the house.

Something more intense that a minor hurricane had been here. Lola knew James would have tied them down well. There were gouges in the pilings where the ropes had rubbed before being torn away.

Roebuck reduced the motor and moved the boat slowly to her father's dock before cutting off the engine. Rene undid his seat belt and removed his earphones. Roebuck moved his set to the top of his baseball cap.

"I don't see a car." Roebuck surveyed the property. Overall, with the exception of the deck, the camp looked structurally sound.

"James always moves his car to a grocery store parking lot with a neighbor's help. Then he uses his boat to get back home." Nodding his understanding, the officer secured the airboat to the dock.

Rene squeezed Lola's hand and jumped onto the dock. They both knew if James was there and able, he would have been waving from the window or already on the dock. Climbing over the smelly grass and other debris, Rene climbed the front steps and used his key to get in. In a matter of moments, Rene called out a broken window that James was not there.

Lola relaxed her shoulders and inhaled deeply. She had not realized she'd been holding her breath. Lola felt a rush when she inhaled deeply the brackish air. Looking up again, she saw her husband using duct tape to secure a file folder over one broken window before moving to cover another. In a short time, Rene was back on the dock.

"Spot's leash and food dish are gone, but his phone charger is still by the bed. I don't see his medicine either. I'm pretty sure he left before the storm and since Ms. Beryl's place is empty, I'd bet they're together." Seeing relief on his wife's face, Rene drew her into an embrace and whispered in her ear, "He's OK Lola."

She hugged her husband back and wiped at the tears that had appeared on her face. Giving him a good squeeze, Lola released him and turned to the officers.

"I'm so sorry we bothered you. After all these years, I can't believe he left without telling us." As she spoke, her concern slowly turned toward irritation.

"That's no problem. We are just glad we didn't find anything serious here."

"Well, he may not be in trouble here, but he will not be happy after I get a hold of him." Lola frowned as she looked back at the damaged home.

"We're losing daylight, so we need to head back," Brown said. Roebuck moved back to his seat on the airboat and checked the controls. Rene sat down and fastened his seatbelt. He leaned over to touch Lola's hand. Just before the engine revved up to speed, she saw him, more than heard him say, 'The Old Coot!" He was smiling, shaking his head.

Lola and her father would be having a conversation. She shook her head and looked toward the open water. *I hope he is enjoying himself now, because he's not going to be happy when I finish giving him a piece of my mind.*

As they picked up speed and started over the water, Lola closed her eyes, gave up a prayer of thanksgiving and enjoyed the feel of the wind in her hair.

*

Katie was seated with her hosts around the picnic table on the patio, enjoying a dinner any carnivore would love. The smoked ribs and brisket had stayed warm in the deluxe cooler sitting on the patio. Lola had used up the last of the fresh vegetables to make a salad. Simple fare for a simple time. On their way home, Rene and Lola had swung by the Marino place to share an update on her wayward father. Patrick and Rose followed them home after an invitation to smoked ribs was extended.

Although the weather had them sporting sweat stains on their t-shirts and hair styles were drooping, it was still a comfortable evening. The breeze left behind by Stella's passing kept the bugs away and provided some relief.

"If we don't get electricity on in the next day or two, we're going to have to drive over to Mississippi to replenish our provisions," Lola mumbled between nibbles on a rib bone.

Weathering the Storm

"Does it usually take long to get the power back?" Katie had finished her plate and refused seconds when Rene offered her the meat platter. As she sat back in the wicker chair, Katie felt content. The other guests were still making appreciative noises as they ate.

"All depends on the level of damage. They tend to focus on places where they can reconnect the most people with the fewest number of repairs first," Rene commented as he tossed another bare rib bone in a large bowl on the table.

When they had returned from their trip on the airboat, the Normandys had taken note of electric company trucks parked near the police station. There was also a crew up in a bucket down the street, replacing the burned transformer. The diners had talked of general storm news throughout their feast.

"It should not be long," Lola stood to clear the table. "They're not far up the road. It can't be too soon. I would pay good money for a shower."

Rene nudged Katie and pseudo whispered to her, "I didn't want to say anything, but she is developing a unique aroma," sending a sideways grin toward his wife.

Patrick suppressed a snort, but otherwise did not comment. *People in glass houses and all.*

"I wouldn't talk," Lola pointed a fork at her husband. "Don't think you smell like a rose just because you've been using that stinky deodorant spray you got on our trip to Scotland."

As Lola moved toward the back door, the back-patio light flickered on overhead. The distinct sound of the air conditioner compressor emanated from the side of the house.

Turning back to the others, Lola whooped.

"Yes, time to shut some windows," Lola called back to them while heading into the kitchen. Rene wiped his mouth with a paper towel and carried a few plates into the house, Katie following in his wake.

Placing her items in the sink, Lola turned on the water faucet and let it sputter until a steady stream poured into the sink. Lola always said she could survive a long time without air conditioning. Not having water flow from a spigot on demand or being able to flush a toilet without hauling water was where she drew the line on roughing it.

Relishing the feel of the water as it poured into the sink, the beeping red light on the answering machine caught her attention. Turning off the tap, she used the kitchen towel to dry her hands while moving to the other counter. Rose and Katie entered the kitchen, carrying the leftovers into the kitchen. Pressing the play button, she heard a welcome voice.

"'Lola. This is your father. Beryl and I are heading out on a little trip. We'll call you when we're settled. Thought you'd be glad to know we are both off the water and Spot is with us. Take care. Love ya.'

Lola bent over the counter with her forehead resting on her clasped hands. That's how Rene found his wife after Katie excitedly motioned him into the kitchen.

"Lola?" Seeing her like that, concern creeped into his voice. "Honey?"

"He decided to take a road trip." Raising her head from the countertop, a lopsided grin formed on her lips as she moved toward her husband. "The crazy man is somewhere on the road with Ms. Beryl."

After walking into his arms, Rene hugged her tight as silent tears fell down her cheeks. *All would be well.* Lola was a rock when times were tough. It was when a crisis passed that she would finally take a moment to let herself go.

"Maybe they went to Vegas," Rose said, knowing Lola was always curious about how serious the relationship was between her father and his neighbor.

Wiping her face against his t-shirt, Lola raised her head and removed herself from her husband's embrace.

"I can't believe he finally listened. The one time I didn't have to worry about him, I didn't get the damn message." Lola shook her head and moved to her purse. She looked up his cell number on her phone and tried calling. It went straight to the message saying he never set up

Weathering the Storm

his voice mail. After putting her phone away, Lola walked back to the sink and started rinsing the plastic food containers.

Dad will call, hopefully sooner rather than later. The warm water rinsed the dishes in the sink. She thought of the TV program her kids used to watch about a young adventurer.

Humming the theme song, Lola wondered, 'Where in the world is Carmen Santiago?' She laughed to herself. Too bad 'James Coubillion' didn't rhyme with the lyrics.

*

Sitting on the pier, Beryl and James rocked quietly as golden birch leaves floated by on the water's surface. The ripples on the surface of Table Rock Lake reflected a multitude of colors as the sun made its descent for the day. The slow rhythm of the swing built for two matched their breathing, content and relaxed. Beryl's left hand rested in James' right one on his knee. James slowly rubbed his thumb over the new gold band sitting there. A matching ring caught the light on his other hand.

"You need to try to call Lola again." Beryl let her foot touch the pier to push off again.

"I will. When I tried this morning, her phone was still out." James' cellphone had died the first night they were in Branson. He had left the charger behind when he left. Rene's ribbing about the ancientness of his phone came back to haunt him when they couldn't find a matching charger at any of the local stores. He could still see the smirk on the young salesman's face when he placed his phone on the counter. *Insolent pup,* James had thought.

Besides just checking in, James had news he needed to share with his daughter and son-in-law and the rest of the family.

*

While their courtship had been long, James and Beryl's engagement had been brief.

Flying over Branson at dusk, Bennett had played tour guide before having to pay attention to his landing checklist. They saw the lake that dominated the area, beautiful foothills, and enough neon to choke a horse. Beryl had never been to the city and enjoyed the view from the plane's small window. It also took her mind off the size of the plane and the less than smooth ride they had endured. Stella's outer bands had followed them north before finally dying out.

"Any type of entertainment you'd find in Vegas, you'll find here. There's even a wedding chapel if you two decide to tie the knot." Their pilot joked through the microphone headset as he banked the plane.

Sitting in the right seat, James gave his friend a look of chagrin.

"Kind of old for that sort of thing, don't you think?" James spotted the long rows of white lights on the horizon as the ground slowing rose up toward the plane.

"Maybe, maybe not," Bennett answered. "With the right woman, marriage can be a good thing. Sure beats snuggling with a hound for warmth on a cold night." The widowers shared a silent moment. Bennett's wife had died more than a decade ago. Both men had talked before about the loneliness when whiskey had flowed freely on previous hunting trips.

"Don't let Lucy hear you say that," James told his friend.

"Never," Bennett chuckled, as a call from the control tower come over the radio.

*

The seed had been planted in James' mind months before. The marriage comment during their flight was a virtual shot of Miracle-gro. Driving around the area the next day, James and Beryl passed the chapel on their way to get a custard sundae.

Sitting at a picnic bench in the shade of a gloriously crimson maple tree, James looked across the table at Beryl.

Weathering the Storm

"How about we get married?"

The creamy custard and drop of hot fudge dripped from her spoon as it had stopped midway from the bowl to her mouth.

"Excuse me?" She put the spoon back in the bowl and slowly used a napkin to wipe up the spill on the table.

James would admit the statement had come out sounding slightly cavalier. Upon further consideration, he liked the idea more by the minute. The second time James said it, it was a definite statement made looking straight into Beryl's eyes.

"Let's get married."

"Married? Over the years, Beryl had learned James was a no-nonsense kind of guy. Once he thought through a decision, he acted. Spontaneous, however, was not a word she would have used to describe him.

"Why not? It makes sense." James tapped the table with his index finger while making each of his points. "We're together almost every day. Our families get along. We enjoy a lot of the same things. We make a good team."

When he had finished his list, Beryl picked up her spoon and took a bite from the melting sundae. She did not disagree with what he said, and she adored the man. A sigh escaped her lips as she swirled her spoon and made the bowl's contents look like mud.

"Beryl?" He hadn't expected a school girl scream or histrionics, but James had thought the woman would show more enthusiasm than this.

Hearing the offer, she had hoped would one day come, Beryl wondered if that was all he saw in her. A teammate? Beryl understood she was a romantic at heart and she was seated across from a pragmatist. Beryl had known that for years. Still she had hoped for more hearts and sonnets when she had dreamed about a proposal from this man. Was that too much to hope for? While her insides quivered, Beryl took a deep breath and looked into James' face.

"Why get married? Truthfully James, with the items you just listed, you could invite me to join your Kiwanis chapter." She looked down and stared at the spoon moving in her hand.

James looked at the woman who had become such an important part of his life over the past two years. Reluctantly, he realized there were probably some things they both knew to be true, but James couldn't recall ever putting them into words. He was guessing this would be a good time.

He reached across the wooden table and picked up Beryl's hands in his. Looking down at them, they were the hands that had helped him pull his crabs from the bayou and bandaged his ankle when he tried to prove he was a much younger softball player. They were the fingers that moved through his hair to calm him on nights when he had trouble falling asleep.

"Beryl," his voice started out low. She leaned a little across the table to hear him better.

"You make me happy. I don't know how to be clearer than that." He saw a smile break across her face. "Well, I guess I can. I do love you Beryl. When you're not with me, there's something missing and I don't feel whole until you are with me again. Marry me. I promise to spend my days making you happy you took a chance on me." James squeezed her hands tight and felt her squeeze back.

"Well." Beryl paused. *There's the hearts and sonnets.* She looked from their clasped hands to James' face. "I am getting a little tired of hauling supper from my house to eat on your deck," she said with a grin. "You make me pretty happy too. Yes James, I'll marry you."

For a moment they just sat at the table, holding hands while sunshine filtered through the bright leaves overhead. After a moment, James stood up and leaned over the table. Without releasing her hands, they sealed the deal with a kiss.

Releasing her, he started to clear the table.

"Get a move on Missy; we have a wedding to get to." James moved toward the parking lot and tossed the trash into the stone waste can. For Beryl, reality began to return to their little daydream.

Weathering the Storm

"What, today? You want to get married today?" She looked up dumbfounded at James. *I know he has little patience for waiting once he makes a decision, but really.*

"Again, why not? I think we can get it done today if we can get the license." He stepped over to the table where she still sat. Helping her to her feet, James grinned at her before pulling her into a tight hug. He beat down to whisper in her ear. "Beryl, if we can, let's get married today. I don't want to waste another day."

Beryl held on tight to the man in her arms. "What about the kids? Don't you want them with us for the ceremony?"

"You're the only one I need to be there. Lola will understand. What about Tony? Will he be mad?"

Beryl thought of her only child. He would not mind.

"I'm sure Tony would like to be here, but their schedules are so busy, and they live so far away." Stepping out of the embrace, Beryl grabbed his arm and squeezed.

"Let's get married today," she said. They both laughed as they walked toward the car.

*

After getting directions from the custard shop manager, the couple drove to the county courthouse. Filling out the paperwork, they attested that they were over the minimum age of fifteen years. "Really? What are they thinking?" James mumbled to Beryl. Walking over to the counter, they showed their IDs and paid the marriage license fee.

Next stop was to a jewelry shop recommended by the court clerk and simple matching gold bands left the store in a small velvet box.

On hour later, James and Beryl stood inside the small, white chapel they had seen from the plane. Bennett, as best man, preened like a rooster in front of his flock. He had joked with the minister that it took a natural disaster to get these two to make it official. The minister's wife stood next to the bride as the second witness. Dressed in the shorts and polo shirts they had worn to sightsee that morning, it made for a rather casual wedding portrait.

But as in wedding pictures across the globe, the bride was radiant as she smiled into the face of her new husband. James looked down at Beryl like he had won the lottery.

*

After closing the window in the guest room, Katie lay supine on the bed. She relished the cool air coming out of the vent as it was moved by the ceiling fan on its highest speed. Her damp clothes added to the change in her body temperature. She was tempted to pull the afghan over her legs. On second thought, she didn't move, deciding to enjoy the chill for a few minutes more.

Staring at the quilt on the opposite wall, Katie mentally prepared to return to her house and the real world. The impromptu vacation Stella had sponsored was coming to an end. The reprieve from her alarm clock, her parent's worried texts and unknown test results was over.

Tomorrow, Katie would call the phone number she was given when the office closed to see when she needed to report to work. She reasoned it would probably be a few days since her boss and the other people who had been able to evacuate would need time to return home. She'd also place a call to Dr. MacDermitt to see they had been able to contact the surgeon's office about scheduling the lumpectomy. The past few days had been busy enough to give her a short reprieve from thinking about her upcoming surgery. *That's something to thank Stella for.* Katie got up off the bed and grabbed her tote bag.

Seeing her Tennessee hat on the dresser, Katie remembered she could also thank the storm for putting a certain air conditioner repair guy/policeman in her path. Katie could admit to herself she was a little excited about the possibility of receiving a phone call from Jake Mesch. It was a bright note in the face of her upcoming surgery. Katie made a vow to herself that she would do her best to not think about a troublesome diagnosis until it became a reality. For now, she'd just be a young woman looking forward to seeing a certain phone number pop up on her cellphone screen.

Tucking her beat-up orange and blue ball cap in her bag, Katie continued to pack.

*

Stella directed her travels toward the northeast. She had passed by Rienville in the dead of night and left behind tokens from the drama she created. As her attitude quieted, Stella made amends for some of her bad behavior by nourishing some farmers' fields in Tennessee with a gentle rain.

The End

Photo by Mark Smith/Pheauxtography

Suzie Bronk Hunt

Suzie Bronk Hunt counts herself a simple Polish girl from Wisconsin who fell in love with a man with Cajun roots. Moving south, she adopted her community in Southeast Louisiana as her own.

A former writer and columnist for the New Orleans Times Picayune, she has put a few words to paper and enjoys sharing a good story with others.

When not working on her next book, Suzie can be found directing a lawn chair brigade, planning her latest road trip or waiting for the Cubs game to come on the radio.

Weathering the Storm

38293648R00114

Made in the USA
Lexington, KY
07 May 2019